The Music of Life

Marcus Blake

~ The Marcus Blake Collection ~

The Music of Life

A Mavericknes Media / Truesource Publishing book

The Music of Life was edited by
Carol Felder and J M Almgreen

The story is fictional and any resemblance to actual
people, places, and certain facts associated with the
characters created by Marcus Blake is purely
coincidence.

Mavericknes Media : Dallas Texas

Truesource Publishing : Dallas Texas

www.truesourcepublishing.com

ISBN : 978-1-932996-58-6

Printed in the United States of America
Published in Dallas, Texas

For More information on Marcus Blake go to....

www.marcusblake.net
www.facebook.com/themarcusblake
www.twitter.com/marcusblake
www.thatnerdshow.com

This Book is dedicated to her for helping me see The Music of Life.

About the Author

    Marcus Blake was born in Chicago, Illinois in 1977. He grew up in Chicago and East Texas. His education is in History, Literature, Psychology, and Religion & Philosophy. Marcus Blake has studied at many universities throughout the United States, but his Alma Mater is Stephen F. Austin State University in Nacogdoches, Texas, which is also where he wrote his first book, The Music of Life. Marcus Blake is a Poet, Musician, Comedian, Writer, and Historian. His books are The Music of Life, My Reflections, Returning Home. Sex Game. The Lonely Girl, Stories From Wrigley, 30 Minutes: Trust and Lies, 30 Minutes: Guilty Until Proven Innocent, 30 Minutes: A Soldier's Song, and 30 Minutes: A Badge of Honor. . He has taught in the public school system, served in the Army, and been a guest speaker at Education and Literary events throughout the world. Marcus Blake is also a Radio Host, his current show is Saturday Morning Nerd Show which can be heard on Saturday Mornings at www.thatnerdshow.com. He is a veteran of Rock and Roll shows as well as Political shows on the radio. Marcus Blake makes his home in the Dallas, Texas.

OTHER BOOKS BY MARCUS BLAKE...

My Reflections

Returning Home

Sex Game

The Lonely Girl

Stories From Wrigley

30 Minutes: Trust and Lies

30 Minutes: Guilty Until Proven Innocent

30 Minutes: A Soldier's Song

30 Minutes: A Badge of Honor

Ring of Warriors: Making a Fighter

My First Novel

"The Music of Life"

It's been nearly twenty years now since I wrote my first novel and it seems like yesterday that I was struggling through my first paragraph while trying to write the greatest novel ever written in just a few sentences. To say that I was ambitious, but naïve, and getting myself into something to which I had no clue about, would be an understatement. But I got through the journey of writing my first novel and once that happened, my life changed forever. It is an interesting thing when your first novel is done because you feel like you can do anything, but at the same time you're the most critical of yourself, wondering if what you've written is any good and then there's the constant feeling of wanting to change everything because it's not good enough. However, eventually you get it done and then it becomes easier to write the next one and the one after that. Six books later it has been an incredible journey so far.

No matter how many stories a writer tells in their lifetime, I think they have that one special story that carries a lot of personal meaning for them. *Returning Home* has meaning for me because it's about my family and has a personal touch to it. And

Sex *Game* has a lot of meaning mainly because it was banned and considered controversial; to this day I still don't even know why. *The Music of Life* is the story that means the most to me. Part of the reason is because it's my first book and the first mark I made on the literary world, but the main reason is because of what the story is about.

I wrote the story when I was 21 years old as a way to tell people what I was really looking for in life. It wasn't that I really wanted to be a professional writer or try to make it as a professional piano player at that time. I was searching for what really made me happy and what I was truly passionate about just like the characters in the book. That's not an easy question to answer when you're that young because in a lot of ways we still haven't figured it out yet at that age. For me at that time in my life I did know one thing with certainty, the only way that I could succeed in life and not become like the tragic characters that I write about was to spend the rest of my life doing what made me completely happy.

It just turned out that I was happier writing stories. We come to a point in our life where we find what makes us happy and we face the choice of whether we can get past the critics, our own fears, and the traps of practicality so in the end we can have the strength to do what makes us happy. Then that's when we have to ask ourselves, do we have the courage to go after what we really want in life? Looking back I think that's another reason I wrote the book and have been writing ever since.

The story behind *The Music of life* is based on real events even if the setting is fiction. The characters represent people that made a profound impact on my life and this is even truer of the person to whom the book is dedicated. I don't know if the outcome of something is always important, but what really matters is what we do to get there. Can we learn from our mistakes, do we have the courage to go after what we really want in life, and can we really make the right choice when faced with second chances compared to the easy, selfish choice that stares us in the face? All of these are the central themes of *The Music of Life* and they are some of the most important themes in the life that we live.

I've lived these themes and will live them again just like everybody else. This is another reason why *The Music of Life* is a special story for me. I can't say for sure which is better, the play or the novel, but the story is still powerful either way with its light humor, dramatic tones, and "Capraesque" essence. The truest thing I discovered when I first wrote this book is that life moves up and down, and we have our times of humor with our times of sorrow or drama just like the notes in a song, hence *The Music of Life*. This makes me wonder what the next ten, twenty, or even fifty years will hold for me, after all the last twenty years have been an interesting ride and believe it or not I'm looking forward to see what the future holds.

My one wish with this story has always been that anybody who reads it will find the inspiration to go after what makes them happy just like I did when I was 21 years old and live their life with that passion. I hope that whoever reads this book enjoys this story as much as I do and when you're done reading you will hear "The Music of Life."

~ *Marcus Blake*

Table of Contents

1

The Remembrance of Her

Somewhere there is a place that we all go in order to retreat from the worries and stressful events of our everyday lives. Hidden among the old buildings and historic neighborhoods of Chicago's North side resides this kind of magical place where searchers and troubadours find peace among friends and soft musical melodies even if it's just for an evening. This place is called *The Blue's Note* and the club is located just a few streets over from De Paul University. It is a favorite to many of the University's students and Chicago's jazz/blues musicians. Many of these musicians have been playing their song for decades in the club lending their own musical voice to the heaven like place.

The club doesn't look much from the outside, just an old weathered building with dirty windows and neon sign that says "live music." The inside isn't very big and the wooden floors creak with the same tempo of the notes being played by the musicians on stage. The bar is square and sits in the middle of the building while the low-lit stage sits in the corner, but it is the center of the club. The magic of the place resides in the people that grace it with laughter and joy, good whiskey, and a yearning for good music.

The Blue's Note has been owned by the same man for over thirty years. A man who had only known one trade his entire life. He's worked in some sort of restaurant and bar all of life. His name is Richard Wilson, but everybody just calls him Bud. His passions are simple, his lovely wife of forty years, the club, and the people that work in it, and of course the bluesy jazz melodies that flow in and out of it every night. He became an old man in the club, some say over night, but its his friend that reminds him of the young man he used to be when he plays the piano for friends and strangers at *The Blue's Note.*

The piano player is Rick and he started playing piano there many years before when he was in high school. He was just a tall lanky kid who discovered his love of music and the sweet sound of the piano in the club. As soon he started playing in the club he knew he was home and Bud, never having a son of his own, knew he would become family. Bud would end up taking care of him being the father figure in his life after his alcoholic mother was killed in a car accident.

Over the years, there have been many forms of entertainment at the club, but it has never quite been that entertaining unless Rick was playing the piano for all of those in search of a good song. The same crowd graces the place almost every night except for a few new faces from the university and surrounding neighborhoods; like most clubs that's how it usually is at *The Blue's Note*. Every spring and fall always brings new faces to the little club and there are always some that leave, forever changed by its magic. To some, as strange as it might sound, this is family to Rick and they always bring out the best in him and his art.

However, out of all the misfit regulars that come in and out of the club there are two men who serve as Rick's best friends and brother like companions. They are Chad and Charlie, brothers and complete opposites, but comrades in arms from the moment they were born. They all grew up in the same neighborhood and met in grade school. The three of them were never apart from one another ever since the first day they met and started their adventures together.

Chad and Charlie were not musicians or athletes unlike Rick, but they became businessmen always finding something to sell to consumers even if it was not theirs to sell. While Rick became a basketball star and musician Chad and Charlie found other pursuits to make money when they were grown men. However no matter what, they were the best of friends hanging out almost every night at the one place that made sense to them, *The Blue's Note*.

Now there are many places like this where it just makes sense to the people that inhabit it, but *The Blue's Note* is where their sordid story takes place. It's the story that allows its characters to find a sense of who they are while finding their own meaning of life. For the regulars who come in every night and the people who own the club they find what makes them happy and through all their pains and sorrows find what makes their lives worth living. Now this is the end result of the story, but there is a beginning, a time and place where the lives of these characters take an honest turn especially for main character of this story.

Rick allowed this notion to enter his thoughts as he sat at the piano with a glass of whiskey reading a letter from her. He had read the letter about a dozen times trying to make sense out of it and trying miserably to hide his pain. At the same time he was happy for her because she was happy living her dream and finding out who she really was as an art student in Paris France. Rick stared at the picture of her in front of a French Jazz Club while sighing with the weight of the world on his shoulders.

Bud came out of the cellar with some beer and wine and saw Rick reading the letter by the piano. He asked him with a grumble in his voice "So did you get another letter from her today?"

Rick Replied to Bud. "Yeah I did, and this time she sent a picture of herself in front of a Jazz club. I guess she wanted to let me know that Paris had good music too and she wasn't being deprived of it."

"Well how is she doing?" "She seems to be doing fine; according to her letter she's having a blast living out her dream. "

"Uh oh, I know that tone."

Rick looked at Bud with a sarcastic look and replied back. "What tone?"

"It's your regretful tone'. You always get it every time she sends you a letter or someone mentions her name. It's that 'I'm not sure if I made the right decision' tone."

"Look, I've told you before Bud. It was the right thing to do. As much as I wanted her to stay or she wanted me to go with her to Paris, I had to let her go."

"Okay, if that's what you have to tell yourself."

"Rick kind of smirked at Bud and then replied. "She wouldn't have been happy if she stayed, and I wouldn't have been happy leaving even if it was with her. It just wasn't time for us to be together so no matter how regretful I might sound; I still think I made the right decision, but that won't ever stop me from reflecting back."

Bud smiled as Rick went back to sipping his whiskey and looking at the picture again Bud replied "Hey, you're the only one that has to convince yourself of that."

Rick just laughed to himself as Bud went back behind the bar to stock beer and wine. He knew his friend was right and it was in the comfort of that true statement that would allow Rick to find his inspiration, to play a great set that night. Rick said to himself.

"Yeah, there's nothing like reflecting back on the past to find your inspiration." Then he went back into his thoughts to remember how this whole story started.

2

That One Perfect Day

One Year earlier...

Rick was really jamming that night with the two horn players and a bass player that made up the night's jazz band. He finished his first set of the night as the club was starting to get busy with the usual characters and wandering strangers looking for a night out. There was a pretty good crowd sitting around the bar while Bud and Susan, the cocktail waitress, were busy trying to keep up with the demands of thirsty customers

Rick put his music away for the time being and walked off stage to help with customers from behind the bar. The regular crowd was seated around the bar having their usual philosophical conversations about life especially Chad and Charlie. Rick smiled and laughed at the two brothers arguing over some mundane subject matter – it was another unimportant conversation for them. He had known them for twenty years and they hadn't changed a bit.

Chad and Charlie might have been siblings but they were day and night to each other and they always took advantage of the other's different temperament when it came to business and pleasure as brother's tend do. Those kinds of moments always caused a lot humor among their friends especially when it added to some kind of trouble they were in, which most of the time was with the law. Their mother, Janet, was a court clerk for a Chicago municipal judge. For Chad and Charlie it helped that their mother was good friends with this judge as much trouble as they got into. When she died the judge promised to look after Chad and Charlie and that helped keep them out of jail.

While the boys were growing up Janet had always had a soft spot for Rick. She was a feisty, stubborn Italian woman who never let anybody get the best of her, but just like her boys Rick could melt her heart. It happened to be this way because he was well mannered and a best friend to Chad and Charlie, always getting them out of trouble when they needed it. Mostly she felt sorry for Rick and took him in when he needed to get away from his alcoholic mother. Like Chad and Charlie Rick never knew who his father was and Janet was always the mother he should have had. When his mother died she let him live with them until he was old enough to be on his own and when she died he shared an equal load of the sorrow with his two best friends Chad and Charlie.

As Rick walked behind the bar to get himself a drink and greet the usual crowd that was sitting on bar stools he couldn't help but think of Janet. He wondered what she would say if she heard the conversation going on by her boys. Rick immediately walked into a conversation his two best friends were having with Bud. Chad and Charlie were having one of their usual philosophical discussions that really had to do with nothing. But no matter what, they were entertaining and always kept anybody who was willing to listen laughing. Conversations like that were not uncommon in this little club and it was a usual take away from anything serious that could be talked about. Rick walked to the corner of the bar where they were sitting just as Chad was going into his narrative

Chad replied in his lecturer's tone "You know what's really wrong with the world today, the problem is 'isms,' and you know what, I don't wanna have anything to do with them."

"So let me get this straight," Charlie replied in his usual cynical tone towards his brother, "you're now saying that everything wrong with the world has to do with isms. Yesterday you said that everything would be okay in the world if everybody was Catholic and the Catholic Church was the only church in the world."

Chad replied. "Well everything would be okay in the world if everybody was Catholic, but also there's the problem of isms."

Bud, laughing out loud said. "I am almost afraid to ask, but what's the problem with the world and isms?"

Chad looked at Bud with a serious look and in a sarcastic tone said. "Well I'm glad you asked because the problem is that everything has got one and that means everything has to be categorized. And we all know that when things get categorized they become bad. Do you realize that to succeed in life you have to be in the right category? Why does everything have to be organized anyway…why can't we leave things just the way they are, you know a little chaos or anarchy and a few nut jobs never hurt anybody and it helps keep the balance in life."

His brother Charlie asked him. "Is there anything resembling normal discussion on the planet you're from? Do you realize most of these philosophical questions of yours never make any real sense? I don't think there's a scientist that could even begin to figure how your mind works or how you think of stuff like this."

"It's probably something that will never be figured out and if it weren't for people like me thinking of things like this then we would all be living in an X-Files episode. Just think about it."

Rick rolled his eyes and replied in a sarcastic tone to Chad. "Well I think that you have a long way to go before you find the truth that's out there. Also I think this theory of yours is just your way of trying to justify the way you make your living."

"There is nothing wrong with how I earn my way in this categorized world. Besides, Charlie and me, we supply the things that other people can't get anywhere else."

Rick looked at him for a moment and with a serious look said. "Let's see, you rip off flea markets convincing the people who own them that they're selling worthless crap just so you can sell the same stuff out of your van at a very much inflated price. Plus you also scalp tickets which are sold at a very high price. Don't you think that's a little dishonest and scrupulous? "

"We only take the stuff that other flea markets are going to throw out anyway and we sell tickets to those who weren't lucky enough to get them at other places, somebody in this world has to do it. "

Rick chuckled. He said. "The world in some weird way wouldn't be better off if there weren't people like you, and I do mean that."

Charlie replied to Rick before Chad could say anything "You know there are people in this world who are suppliers, some people who are producers and some people who are just buyers; me and Chad we're just suppliers. At least that's what Father O'Brian told me the other day when he asked us to get him *Phantom of the Opera* tickets."

"I bet drug dealers consider themselves suppliers as well, what do you think?" Rick said in a sarcastic tone.

"Maybe, but we don't supply anything that kills anybody therefore we don't break any commandments. You're the one that is selling stuff to people that will eventually kill them so you're worse than I am."

"Yeah, but we do it legally and it's really the government's fault for allowing us to sell stuff that might kill people. So whose fault is that?"

Both men just laughed as they usually did when they found a moral loophole for the things they did. It was just part of the game that they played every day. It had to do with something they liked to call "anything goes in a bar." As they all continued their conversation Chad looked up and saw four women walk in together. He gestured and made everybody take notice by tapping them and pointing at the women walking in.

None of the women looked familiar so it became obvious that it was their first time at the bar. Rick, Chad, Charlie, and Bud knew just about everybody that walked in. The four women took a seat at a table near the stage as all the guys watched in curiosity.

The women looked serious, the type that knows only business, but nothing of pleasure. Three of them had short to medium- short business hair cuts that offered nothing of seduction or sensuality. While all the men at the bar stared at them as they walked through the club to their seats there was one in the group that caught Rick's eye. She was younger looking and a very beautiful redhead with very sweet simple green eyes.

She was tall and fair, with a graceful innocence that added to her beauty, but it was not these features that caught Rick's eye. It was her smile for it was full of life and something that could inspire even the most cynical of characters. He did not stop looking at her as she took her seat until somebody at the bar spoke up.

Chad while looking at the girls replied with a joyful tone. "Cool we've got some lesbians here tonight; it's not often that we get lesbians here for us to watch."

Charlie responded. "Look you giant pervert do you think gay women are some feature attraction for
us to get our jollies off at? Just cool off there peewee hormone, it's not that much to get excited about."

Rick started laughing at his friends comments and replied. "How do you know that they're lesbians? You can't tell if a woman is a lesbian by the way she looks!

Besides we probably get them in here all the time and you never notice.”

“Hey what about Cindy Williams you can definitely tell she’s gay by the way she looks” Charlie said to Rick.

“Okay that’s because she looks more like a man than both you and me so it’s easy to assume that she likes women, and frankly that assumption just happens to be right about her.”

Before Charlie could say anything Chad spoke up and replied “Trust me I know a lesbian when I see one and when four women walk in together without a man they have to be gay.”

“Chad, you really are just a simple minded creature aren’t you,” replied Rick.

All Chad could do was smile at his friend. He took a big drink of beer to gain his confidence, stood up, and winked at Rick. He patted his brother on the back as he walked towards the four women sitting at the table. Chad was determined to flirt with them in his own weird way. Mostly he just wanted to have some fun with them because it was not often that *The Blue’s Note* got visitors of their kind or so he thought.

Rick shook his head and laughed then he said. “Great, it looks like I’m going to have to stop him from making a fool out of himself and driving our customers away.... again."

"And how's that different from any other night." Charlie said.

"He's your brother, you should know how to stop him when he gets this way."

"I've been trying for nearly thirty years and the only conclusion that I've come up with is that there is no cure; we just have to wait for his species to become extinct."

Chad walked up to the table that the four women were sitting at while checking his hair like a bumbling geek. All four women look at him at the same time with the same surprised look trying to figure out what crazy, cheap romantic line he would give them. Chad had a weird and sarcastic look on his face and then while standing at the edge of their table, holding a beer in one hand, he spoke, spewing a satirical jargon that they had never heard before.

Chad said. "So how are you chicks doing, can I get you something to drink even though I'm not the right type for you?"

Amanda, one of the three serious looking women responded back to Chad. "Sir we don't know what you're implying, but we didn't come here to be harassed by some local that thinks of himself as a 'real ladies man'..."

"Hey it's okay I'm not trying to pick you up or anything. You know I had a cousin that was a lesbian and she was cool as hell; I loved hanging out with her."

"Congratulations on your cousin, but you're not assuming that we're lesbians are you?"

"Well the four of you came walking in together without a man and you're sitting pretty close to one another. Besides, some of you have short haircuts, so doesn't that mean you're gay.

The three serious looking women got angry at Chad's poor assumptions. The other woman at the table started to laugh quietly as the other three had horrified looks and were looking for something to throw at him. Her name was Elizabeth, but everybody called her Liz. She had a great sense of humor and never let anything bother her. It was this kind of attitude that allowed her to find the whole situation humorous instead of getting angry.

Before the women could find anything to throw at Chad, Rick walked up to the table. Before Rick could say anything Clara, one of the other serious looking women replied. "You have got to be kidding! You think that just because four women are together and some have short haircuts they're gay?"

Chad responded. "Hey it's okay; if you're cool with it then I am certainly cool with it. It just so happens I'm a lesbian, I mean I love chicks and sometimes they even like me. I just wanted to buy you a drink since I happen to know the owner of the place and also I wanted to see if you wanted to have some fun."

Rick: slapped Chad on the back of the head for his comment as the three women got even angrier. Liz didn't though, she just started laughing even more.

Rick to the women at the table "Ladies I'm sorry if he's bothering you; I'll make him go sit back in the corner again while he finishes his time-out. I don't want you to think that this sort of thing happens here all the time, and since I'm a person in charge let me know if there is anything I can do to make your stay more enjoyable."

Michelle, other serious woman replied to Rick. "I don't suppose you could shoot him for us, but you probably wouldn't do that since it looks like he's a friend of yours."

"Ma'am we have similar thoughts about him almost every night and yes, he's a friend, but that's just because he ignores the restraining order we have out against him so there isn't anything else we can do except be his friend."

"That's not a good excuse... I would be ashamed to have someone like him as a friend."

"Hey, everybody needs a friend I guess. All jokes aside though, I will make sure he won't bother you again and I'll get a round of drinks for you on the house."

Rick turned to his friend Chad and replied. "It's time for you to go back to the bar now, they're not interested in you."

"I don't see why not; I'm a gorgeous guy. I don't see what they have to be mad about."

"I'm sure it was the lesbian remark considering they're not really gay. The other thing is when you flirt with women it comes off pretty sleazy."

"I didn't say anything that wasn't true, but you see it just goes to show that you can't call a chick a babe anymore." The four women heard Chad's remark and of course the three serious women started to say something in disgust, but Liz stopped them. Instead they just gave Chad a dirty look.

"Go sit down before I have to hit you."

The Women thanked Rick for getting Chad away from their table and directing him back to his seat at the bar. Rick went back to bar to make them their drinks. As he was doing so he looked and said. "Alright, I just got you out of trouble again; don't bother them anymore or any other guest. If you keep this up I will revoke your talking privileges for the night... again."

Before Chad could say anything Charlie spoke up and said "You see, this is why I can't bring women over to our place. You can't keep your mouth shut and you're a constant embarrassment." Charlie looked around the bar and asked everyone. "So anyone want to bet he loses his talking privileges tonight like last week?"

Within a matter of seconds, people sitting around the bar started placing their bets with Charlie and all Rick can do was laugh. This was not unusual because everybody liked to make some sort of wager on how Chad was going to embarrass himself during any given night at the club. He was a source of comedic entertainment for the patrons, but not matter what it was always in good fun and brought about some good times at *The Blue's Note.*

Even Bud had to start laughing at what Charlie was doing.

He replied. "You know there are some things that never change around here." He looked at Rick and said. "Before you started playing here years ago this would have seemed strange." Then Bud just walked off to the other side of the bar.

Rick gathered his drinks and walked back to the table that the four women are sitting at. He never took his eye off of Liz while walked up to the table. He was enchanted especially since she was a simple girl who liked to drink beer for that's what she ordered. It was good beer too, not some cheap watered down American beer, but one that you could actually taste. To say he was attracted to her by now would have been an understatement.

Rick replied to the women as he put their drinks on the table."My name is Rick and I usually provide the entertainment around here. I can't say that I have ever seen you in here before."

"It's nice to meet you," Liz replied back. "My name is Liz and this is Clara, Michelle, and Amanda; Amanda is the director of the Chicago office for PETA. Are you a supporter of PETA Rick?"

"I never gave much thought about it because we don't get any abused animals around here unless you count Chad, but that's only because we abuse him being one of our regular customers and all."

The other three women were now starting to get annoyed at Rick and his sarcastic comments. Finally Amanda spoke up and replied. "You think that's funny? PETA is a very serious organization, and what we do for the ethical treatment of animals is no laughing matter. I hope you're not as despicable as your friend over there."

Rick said to her. "Well I'm not, and I thought I was pretty funny, but talking with you has made realize that I'm not and there is a very serious issue of abused animals, especially here in Chicago Blue's Clubs."

Liz started laughing at him while the other three all gave Rick dirty looks for his remarks. Rick said. "I'm sorry for being too sarcastic. I've had fun talking with you, but I do have to do my next set since I am the piano player. Please come back again and I hope you do enjoy the music."

Rick walked back to the stage and took a seat behind the piano. The band warmed up and then they all started to jam. While Rick played he still couldn't take his eyes off of Liz and she couldn't stop staring at him. He was really in his groove. Since he was in a place where the best of his art was coming out he decided to play some of the songs he had not played for a long time. They were some of his favorites, there were very much treasures of the heart and soul.

Amanda looked at Liz with disgust and replied. "I can't believe him and his insensitive remarks; he's just as bad as the other guy. I heard this place was supposed to be fun and one of the best places for good music and drinks on the North Side."

"Well it's certainly entertaining here and you can't blame that guy Rick, he was just trying to be funny and liven up the somber mood you three created. I'm sure he didn't mean anything by his remarks."

Michelle said to Liz. "He's just the type of guy you would fall for; I still can't see why you think sarcasm is a great quality in a guy."

With a sarcastic look Liz said to the three women sitting with her. "Well you get a sense of humor then you'll understand."

Michelle gave Liz a dirty look as the music started. All four of them stopped in the middle of their conversation to listen even though it was only Liz who was really interested. Rick was really on a role and then with a surprise move he played a song that he had not played in a long time – not since his heart had been broken years before. It was an old Sinatra song. He played the song to finish the set glancing at Liz while he played. When he was done for the evening he put his music up and walked back to the bar.

Charlie said to Rick as he walked behind the bar. "Your last song was *The Way You Look Tonight;* there must be a woman in the bar that peaked your interest."

"Charlie you know that's one of my favorite songs and it's just been awhile since I have played it so don't start getting suspicious."

Chad laughed out loud and said. "Yeah, but you don't usually play that song unless it's a request or there's somebody in the audience you're secretly trying to impress. I bet it's one of those four lesbians over there, but I don't know why because it's not like you actually have a chance with them."

"Hey, here's a concept maybe not familiar with; they're really not lesbians, but just ultra liberal feminists that don't like you." Rick said to Chad.

"No we don't usually get those around here, they have to be lesbians. Besides, who could resist a guy like me or at least a guy that would buy someone a free drink? Women love me because I'm happy and handsome."

"Hey Chad, you just keep telling yourself that and you won't have to worry about over-populating this world."

Just as Rick finished his sentence the four women got up to leave. Liz started to walk towards the bar while everybody sitting around it took notice of what she was doing. She walked up to the bar with a confidence that was unusual for young women. She had a smile on her face and stared at Rick every step of the way towards the bar. And just like her, Rick couldn't take his eyes off at the person in front of him.

Liz extended her hand to shake Rick's and said. "I just wanted to thank you for the drinks and tell you that at least one of us had a good time tonight."

Rick with a smile reached out to shake Liz's hand and said. "That's good; hopefully that person will come back. Also, I'm sorry if the sarcasm was a little much, but it tends to be that way around here; it's a bar and anything goes."

"That's okay. You're not that insincere as my so-called friends tried to point out, and you did make up for it by playing one of my favorite songs."

"Which song was that?"

"The song was *The Way You Look Tonight* by Sinatra; my grandmother used to play it on the piano for my grandfather so it became one of my favorite songs because of them."

Rick smiled and said. "Well it's always been one of my favorites too; maybe I can play another song for you sometime if you are willing to come back."

"Who knows, stranger things have happened so I guess we'll see what happens."

The Liz turned around and walked out of the bar, but she turned around just once on her way out to look at Rick again. She smiled at him once more and he winked her. That's all it took for them to be intrigued by each other and somehow Rick knew that he would not see her for the last time. And after hearing about one of her favorite songs being a sweet classic melody he knew without a doubt that there was something about her and it would more than just an attraction for him.

Rick turned around to see everybody staring at him with sarcastic smiles. With the same sarcastic smile he said to all of them. "Nobody say a damn word and I'll even get you a free drink if you can refrain from your comments."

3

Second Chances

It was next day at *The Blue's Note* and the scene from the previous day was exactly the same. The bar was starting to get busy and the same faces were sitting around the bar carrying on their usual conversations. Rick was on stage with the band from the night before about to start his first set. The band was made up of old jazz musicians from the neighborhood, the same jazz musicians that Rick had learned from. One of them in particular was Gus, and old trumpet player who had been blowing sweet melodies for over fifty years in clubs and cat houses. He was a master just like Armstrong and he was a true musician, a traveling troubadour who never settled into the 9 to 5 kind of life.

Gus was Rick's most influential teacher when it came to the music of life; he helped Rick find his true love and the part of himself that would always be true.

Bud was in his usual place, behind the bar making sure everybody had a drink in hand and a place to sit so they could hear the music and for another day forget about their wretched lives. Susan the regular cocktail waitress was her usual self, flirting and laughing with the customers making them feel at home even if the club was the last place they needed to be.

Susan had worked at the club for the last five years, putting herself through college and law school. She was like the daughter Bud never had and he adored even though he never admitted it out loud. She was a very beautiful blond woman, slender and sassy, but full of life. There wasn't a man who came to the club that wasn't a little bit in love with her and she used that to her advantage when it came to making tips.

She had two passions education and the Chicago Cubs, the latter making her one of the boys. She loved baseball because of her dad- he was an old Bleacher Bum from 69'.

Her favorite time to watch Cubs was in the bar with her favorite people, Rick, Bud, Chad, and Charlie. She also loved music, mainly rock, blues, and jazz, which made her adored by Rick and the gang. If there was anything that could make Rick fall in love with her it would be her love of music, but in the end it was never enough for the two of them to make a go of it.

They had a brief intimate history together, but they also knew that any kind of love they had for each other would be best in friendship. Susan would end up being a great friend to all of them. She was family and whether they would all admit to it or not, they would all be better off with the friendships they had with each other. Night after night she flirted, she harassed, and she made life a little bit better for her friends and the patrons of the club with her fun and feisty persona.

While the evening was getting on the way Rick and the band started to play their first set. Half way through the set Liz walked through the door and took a seat at the bar not too far from where the regular crowd was sitting. When she sat down all the regulars who were sitting around the same part of the bar looked up at the same time and stared at her for a moment

Chad tapped his brother Charlie on the shoulder and pointed at Liz smiling with a cocky look as if to say that she was in the bar to see him. Chad smiled at Liz while she ignored him and then Charlie gave his brother a dirty look.

Charlie replied to his brother Chad "Don't get too excited, I don't think that she's here for you. Something tells me Rick has already got the victory when it comes to getting this girl."

"You don't know that, maybe my charm overwhelmed her and she came back in to see me."

"You're right little brother and that's why she's staring at Rick and hasn't come over here to say hi yet."

"She's just playing hard to get."

"You know, mom was right about you; you're just a lost cause when it comes to women. She always said that it wouldn't be surprising if you turned out gay."

"Hey, I am not gay and just because I got caught wearing a dress one time, which I might add was for a Halloween costume…I wanted to look like a member of *Twisted Sister*. That doesn't make me a gay."

Bud walked into the middle of this conversation of Chad and Charlie shaking his head like a disgruntled parent. He stared at the both of them for a moment and he replied in a sarcastic tone. "Well I don't know any straight guys who wear dresses around here do you Charlie?"

"No, can't say that I know any, and besides Chad, we're not judging you in any way. If you want to be gay, that's cool. You'll still be my brother…just my really, really gay brother who likes to wear women's clothes and who is going to hell according to the church."

Rick walked over to the bar after finishing his first set   and hears the last part of the conversation. He starts to laugh and replies "Is Chad trying to prove again that he is not a closet case? You know you should just finally admit that you're gay and quit using the excuse that you have no luck with women."

Everybody around the bar started laughing while Chad gave Rick a dirty look for his comment. Rick grabbed a drink then Chad replied. "All of you can just kiss my ass and I don't have any luck with women around here because none of them understand me."

Rick said to Chad. "You know, I'm just going to leave that one alone because it's just too easy. Also Chad, you should be left to your own delusion."

While everybody started to laugh again, Charlie pointed to the visitor at the bar. Rick looked over and saw Liz sitting alone with her drink. He winked at her and as he left for the stage to start his second set. When he walked past her he said that he was glad she came back and not to leave before he got a chance to talk to her again. Rick and the band didn't play as many songs as they usually did in the second set and the rest of band knew why. Rick wanted to get done as fast as he could so he could talk with Liz.

It had been a long time since Rick had been this excited at the chance to talk with a beautiful woman. There was something about her, something that gave him an inspiring feeling. He didn't what it was yet, but he did recognize it in her. He met beautiful women on a daily basis at the club, but none of them could make him feel the same joy one has when they want to love something more than themselves. For Rick there had only been one person that could make him feel that way and she was also the only one that had broken his heart. When the band was done Rick rushed to put his music away and then quickly walked over to where she was sitting; he was like an infatuated teenager again.

He walked up to her and said. "Well I thought yesterday would be the last time we would ever see you after my friend harassed you and your friends."

Liz replied to Rick. "Oh, he was harmless and I'm sure he's not that bad of a person despite what my so called friend said about him after we left."

"Those people you were with were not really your friends?"

"No, there more like acquaintances; my real friends actually have a sense of humor. The only reason I was with them last night is because I was helping out with their PETA rally yesterday. Anyway I believe in giving people a second chance, and I mean all people."

"Why, thank you; we all deserve a second chance I guess."

Liz gave Rick a sarcastic look, laughed to herself and said. "Oh... I was referring to your friend Chad."

"So was I. I was just thanking you on his behalf."

Bud was cleaning up behind the bar while sort of easy dropping on their conversation. Everybody else just sat there on their bar stools not saying a word and staring intently at Rick as he flirted with this new girl in the in the club. They were all curious about what was going on because they all knew that there must be something about her for Rick to be so interested. It was a rare thing for him to be that interested especially after the only love of his life had walked out on him many years before.

Charlie finally spoke up and said. "Hey Rick not to break up this nice little moment with you two as you cut through all the sexual tension, but don't you think you should quit being rude and properly introduce everybody?"

Rick replied back. "I don't really think you feel all that bad about trying to ruin the mood, but I will indulge you and make the proper introductions." He pointed at each one of them and said to Liz. "Liz, this is Charlie, Chad whom you have unfortunately met last night, and the owner of the bar, Bud."

Liz walked over and shook each of their hands while Susan walked up behind them and said "Now Rick, you're not going to forget me are you," She nudged Rick in the side of his ribs. "You know I would never let you live it down, or I could just ruin this nice moment you have right now by telling her your dirty little past with other women who've come in here."

Rick gave her a dirty look and replied. "Damn, the bitch in you comes out at the most inappropriate times." He looked over at Liz again and said. "This is Susan who has very sharp claws that she likes to dig into anything good when it comes to both men and women, so watch out. You probably wouldn't find it too surprising that she is going to Law School."

Liz and Susan shook hands and then Susan turned around to Rick and smiled. She was giving a look of approval when it came to Liz; she knew better than anybody the type of girl Rick was attracted to and Liz certainly fit the bill. Just as Rick was about to start talking to Liz again this old crusty voice spoke up. It was Old Man Henderson, the resident alcoholic and chauvinist pig. He was harmless though, he never did anything that was really bad or that a woman working for tips didn't let happen to them.

Old Man Henderson, "Hey what about me Rick, I'm in here every day and practically watched you grow up. Aren't you going to introduce me to your new dame?"

Rick said to Liz. "Oh yeah that's Old Man Henderson and he's our ' Norm ' at this club." She asked Rick. "Does he have a first name or do you just call him Old Man Henderson?

"We really don't know what his first name is or if he actually has one. As long as anyone has known him he has been called Old Man Henderson and he has been coming to this bar every day since even before Bud became the owner. Apparently He went to an AA meeting across the street over thirty years ago, stayed five minutes, decided he didn't like it, and then came here. Since then he's never really left."

"Is that a true story or are you just making that up?"

"I don't know if that's true or not, buts it's a funny story regardless and consequently enough the Alcoholics Anonymous chapter across the street has been trying to shut us down ever since. Although, they've forgotten one thing."

"And what's that?"

"People love to drink around here and as long as we are selling the last legal drug that can kill you, people are going to come here like its water in a desert."

"So is there anybody else in the bar I should meet?"

"Well, everybody else is just a regular, and once you've been coming here for a certain period of time, then you just become a regular and names are unimportant. It's kind of like a family I guess."

"Well you definitely have an assortment of interesting characters here. I knew this would be a place I could like as soon as I first walked in the door, unlike those women I was with yesterday."

"If that's the case, then would you like to stay and have a cup of coffee with me after everybody else leaves?"

"I would like that."

It' was about time for the club to close and Rick leaned over to tell Bud that he would finish closing up. Bud told Rick that it was much appreciated and announced that everybody had to finish their drinks and leave. Bud gathered the money out of the cash register and went into the office to count it while Rick made a fresh pot of coffee and washed the last of the glasses. Susan was busy gathering the last of the glasses around the bar for Rick and making sarcastic comments to him about his new lady friend. He just gave her a dirty look and hurried her out from the bar area so she would leave while doing the same to the other remaining patrons.

Rick wanted to get everybody out as fast possible as to avoid anymore comments and so he could finally be alone with Liz. It was much like those embarrassing moments in high school where our friends were always cramping our style and never leaving us alone with a member of the opposite sex. The same kind of friends that harassed you about everything because they were the ones that truly cared about you. Rick finally got everybody out of their seats and moving towards the door including Chad and Charlie.

Chad as he was heading for the door pulled something out of his pocket to hand to Rick and said "Hey Rick, here's something you might need."

"Damn it Chad, it's not like that and I don't need those." Rick said.

Charlie grabbed his brother and pulled him away from the bar towards the door. He said to him."Chad, you really have no idea what tact is do you? For crying out loud you don't give a guy condoms in front of a woman; it just makes him look like a 'perv.' How many times do we have to go through this?"

"What, I was just trying to help the guy out. I didn't mean anything by it." Chad said.

"You never do; that's your problem."

Liz started laughing to herself as Rick shook his head. He took then took the condoms and placed them in a drawer below the top of the bar. Rick replied to Liz. "My friends… they're always looking out for me."

"That's what they're supposed to do even if it is at the wrong time."

Everybody finally left as Susan hurried everybody out the door. As patrons were walking out the door she was telling them out loud to move faster so Rick could make a move on Liz. Rick gave her a dirty look and she just winkled at him before walking out. Rick got Liz a cup of coffee just like he promised for their first date then he went back to washing glasses.

Liz looked at him wondering look and said to Rick "Ever since I met you last night I have been racking my brain trying to figure out where I have seen you. I know you from somewhere."

"Well I'm known throughout the neighborhood and this part of the city since I play piano here almost every night and I grew up around here. I'm also known around campus because we get a lot of college kids in here. Some of them work here part time, but most of them just come to drink."

"Actually that's not it. I did ask one of my professors about this place. After I asked her she asked me if I got a chance to meet the piano player and I'm quoting 'He's really good and shouldn't be playing in a place like that, but more like Las Vegas or Hollywood.'"

"It looks like I have a few fans at De Paul besides the students."

"She also told me that you were a student and played Basketball at De Paul. When I went to find out about you I ran into a Coach Graves, the head coach of the basketball team and he told me all about you."

As kid growing up in the neighborhood he found a love for basketball just as he had for music. From the first moment he placed his hands on the ball and started playing pickup games in the park he found he had a unique talent with a basketball. He had excellent ball handling skills at a young age and he could shoot; playing basketball just came natural like playing piano. He would play against older kids and would beat them gaining a reputation among the courts in the park as a major player.

Basketball was another release for Rick just like music was; it was another way of dealing with not having a father at home and an alcoholic mother. She worked as a secretary and when she wasn't at work she was drunk. There was never enough money around because she would spend it all on booze. When the money ran out and she needed a quick fix there would always be some guy that would give her money for a night's entertainment.

Rick never wanted to be around for that so he did whatever he could to keep himself away and basketball was just one more thing that kept him away from home. His mother had her moments when she could be caring, sweet, and a lot of fun to be around, but it wasn't enough to put up with her drunken games.

Most of the time he would spend time with Chad and Charlie and his mother never cared where he was as long as he wasn't in the way. Eventually she would die when he was in high school leaving everything she had including the apartment to him. He was sixteen and he was already a basketball star leading his high school team to the State Championship two years in a row. He would graduate highs school a year early and have lots of big colleges recruiting him for basketball.

In the end it was Coach Graves from De Paul that helped him the most after his mother died besides his friends. Rick never had any other family besides his best friends and their mother. Coach Graves was the one person who took Rick under his wing and he never tried to get him to come play basketball for him at De Paul. But he did help Rick not make a bad decision when it came to his college career. Rick eventually decided to stay in Chicago and play ball at De Paul with Coach Graves - he stayed because the coach had become family. The coach would help take care of him. While at De Paul Rick stilled played piano at The Blue's Note just like he did in high school making the club part of his home for the rest of life.

After a brief pause Rick finally answered "Yeah, it's true I used to play basketball at De Paul University and that's another reason I'm still known around campus."

Liz with a curious look said. "Coach Graves told me that you were an All-American and you were going to play professional basketball. He also said you were going to be the next Larry Bird."

Rick laughed out loud to himself and then replied to Liz. "I don't know about the next Larry Bird, but everything else is true. I was really good and had a chance to play in the NBA. You did a lot of detective work just to find out about me. Why? What is it about me that's so interesting?"

When I am curious about something, I want to know everything there is to know about it. After Coach Graves told me about you I remembered that I saw you play one time when I was a junior in High School. My father is a huge basketball fan and loves De Paul; he took me to the Conference Championship that year where you hit that winning three pointer to win the game with only one second left on the clock. Honestly, I just want to know why a guy with so much potential is in a place like this."

Rick smiled and paused for moment to see the look upon her face like he had already let her down. He laughed a little more and said to her. " I bet you think that I ended up in this place by accident or because I failed while not having anywhere else to go, but maybe I ended up here on purpose. Besides, I don't really know you well enough to tell you the story. I'm not really sure you would understand."

Liz grabbed his hand and stopped him from moving then looked at him directly in the eye and said. "Everybody has a story they think other people won't understand. Even I have a story that you might not understand, but I'll tell you mine if you tell me yours."

"Well I guess that's fair, but maybe I don't want to tell you my story. It is a little too personal for a first date."

"Is that what this is, a first date? I don't know if I would call this a date. Maybe dinner and movie would qualify as a date instead of sitting in a bar having a cup of coffee with someone who can't answer any of my questions. This is too much of an interview to qualify as a date."

"Liz, all first dates are interviews and if you can conceive that this might be a first date with the possibility of a second date tomorrow then I *will* tell you want you want to know."

"You're not going to make this easy are you?"

"No, but when is anything between men and women easy especially when they first meet each other?"

"I can see I have my work cut for me here, but I'll bite. We can call this a first date if you answer my question."

"I just wanted to make this seem like a first date, so if I actually ask you out for dinner and movie then the awkwardness of a first date would be behind us and we can move right into "dating bliss."

"That's very nice and well thought out Sherlock, but you're still stalling."

Rick couldn't help but smile at her; it was her sassy nature that made him really like her. He already knew that he was going to like her; he knew that they would get along great and have a lot of fun. She liked him as well and she knew that there was something about him that made him special. Rick had a charisma and inspiring way about him that made people want to be better than what they were. She didn't know what it was, she just knew it was there and he had it.

However there was something that he wasn't letting on about himself and she knew it had something to do with his story. It was this thing about him that made people think he was crazy or some kind of failure – somebody that could only be described full of shit. The truth is he was just as full of shit as anybody else, but he had one thing figured out and it was that one thing that nobody could understand except his friends. Because most people could not understand they naturally saw Rick in a negative light. He never minded though, he knew better than anybody that people were going to see what they wanted to see and he couldn't change that. All he could do was be himself and find own way to be happy.

Rick saw that she really wanted to know about what had happened to him so he decided to have a little faith and tell her. First thing was first thought, had to be a little sarcastic towards her – it was part of who he was. He said to her. "You don't cut anyone any slack do you? So just to put you out of your misery, I'll tell you what you want to know, but for some details there will have to be some friendly torture."

"So what you're saying is you like to be dominated? That doesn't happen on the first date for me, but the sky's the limit on the second if you have the nerve to ask me out for real."

"We'll see."

Rick smiled at her and she gave him a dirty look. The both knew that there would probably be a second date; they were already beginning to find out how much they liked each other. Now neither one of them believed in love at first site, but they both believed that you sense something great about another person as well as knowing that there was some kind of an attraction or chemistry. It's the electricity in something that you cannot always see, but you feel it just like you feel the music move you without having to see then notes being played. She gave him a look and a nudge that said that he could continue with his story so he did.

Rick told her about how he grew up in the neighborhood. He told her that the two things he learned how to do well was play the piano and play basketball; it was an odd combination of talents, but they suited him well. Most of his formal education on the piano came from local jazz musicians who've been playing music for most of their lives in this part of Chicago. Coach Graves did try to get Rick to come to De Paul, even though he would later admit he knew he probably never had a chance at getting him to come. Rick told Liz that when his mother died Coach Graves was the only coach to come to the funeral He told Rick he would help him in any way he could even if I never played ball at De Paul.

Liz asked Rick "Is that what made you decide to stay in Chicago and play basketball at De Paul?"

"Yeah, and I knew he would be someone that would do me right. Also, when it really came down to it, I didn't want to leave home."

Liz asked him what happened when he was at De Paul so Rick continued his story and told her. As a basketball player he would be put in the starting lineup halfway through his freshman year. He would later become known as the heart and soul of the team for the three and half years he started for the team. Rick pointed out that he played on some really good teams at De Paul, so good that they went to the NCAA tournament three years in a row, and made it to the final four his junior year before losing to Duke. Duke ended up winning the championship that year. There were a lot of NBA teams that wanted to draft Rick his junior and senior year, but it didn't quite happen that way.

Liz had a very curious and concerned look as Rick was telling his story then she asked him why he didn't go the NBA. Rick continued telling her his saga of how he ended where he did. In his senior year at De Paul he tore two major ligaments in his right knee diving for a loose ball; it was in the first round game during the NCAA tournament that year. After two surgeries he was told by my doctors that he would be lucky to ever walk normal again.

Rick would always laugh at the strange sense of irony with his injury that his chance at professional basketball bounced away with that loose ball and the type of play that made him a great basketball player would also end his career. It would've been really nice if De Paul would have at least won the first round game without me, he told her, but they didn't and my basketball career was over just like that as he snapped his fingers.

Liz gave him a weird look and asked Rick "So you became a piano player slash bartender because you couldn't play basketball anymore? Please tell me there's more to this story than just that."

Rick replied back to her "Oh, my story is not that boring and unoriginal. There's a combination of things that got me here, but what you should know is that this place saved me in more ways than one. I found a saving grace within this place that I call my *Hub in the Universe*."

She replied back. "Your *Hub in the Universe*, what do you mean by that?"

"You never heard that before?"

Liz shook her head no and with a sarcastic look on her face replied. "It sounds like something you made up, but I still want to know what it is?"

"Your "Hub in the Universe" is that one place where you can retreat to so you can feel totally happy and at peace. It can be anything, and the variables of that place will be different for everybody. My place just happens to be a dingy blues and jazz club with a piano in the corner. Not too surprising now that you know me a little bit better, huh?"

"I guess I shouldn't be too surprised, but I don't quite understand why this kind of place is so special; maybe I just need to get to know you better first."

"It may take that before you know the answer, but if you do figure it out let me know, because even I don't fully understand why this kind of place would be my *Hub in the Universe.*"

"You still haven't answered my question on how you ended up here. Do I get to know the answer or do I have to see you again to find out?"

Rick gave her a dirty look and then smiled. He had been stalling a little bit and she caught on. His stalling had nothing to do with not wanting to be honest, he just wasn't sure if Liz would understand without knowing him very well. He stared at her for a moment as she had an intent look on her face waiting for him to finally tell her. Rick finally said to

Liz. "What the hell, I'll tell you, but you still have to see me again tomorrow, deal?"

"Okay, deal. So what happened?"

Rick explained to Liz that after he got injured and couldn't play anymore he was a total wreck and didn't really see the point of living anymore. It was something that everybody feels at some point in their life after a tragedy. Rick started drinking just like his mother; he quit going to class, and didn't do what he needed to do in order to graduate. Also his girlfriend of seven years left him for one of his De Paul teammates who did go into the NBA. Basically Rick ended up at the club most days playing piano for the evening crowd.

Rick gave up on life, his friends, school, and anything that truly mattered. The only thing that saved him was being at *The Blue's Note* playing music every night. The club was the only place where he really felt happy. As a result he became the regular piano player again like he was in high school and a permanent bartender.

Rick would eventually became a partner with Bud at *The Blue's Note*. In no small way he never really left what would become home. For Rick the only family he had left was in the place called *The Blue's Note*. His family was the best friends he ever had, to the musicians that he learned music from in the old neighborhood, and a partner that became the father he never had. Rick for the first time in his life could honestly say that he had found total happiness here in the place that he called home.

After staring at Rick for a moment with an unconvincing look Liz finally asked. "So all the depression you had disappeared because you were in this place? I don't think I've ever heard of that before and I don't know if I can quite believe it."

Rick laughed for a moment and replied back "When you find your *Hub in the Universe*, you'll also find that it also has magical powers that can take away any sadness or depression. I found that here and that's probably why I never left; and as you saw yesterday, it's never a dull moment around here. So now that I've answered your questions, tell me about you and what brings you here."

With Liz there wasn't that much to tell. She was going into her seventh year at De Paul University. Her family was rich because her had dad invested in Microsoft and Intel back in the eighties. He also started his own technology company. When it was all said and done Liz would graduate De Paul with three degrees that year. She didn't really have any idea on what she really wanted to do with her life except for some small dream of becoming an artist. However her father's plan was for her to come and woke at his company doing something she would probably hate doing.

Rick looked at her with a stunned look and replied to her "Wow, three degrees, and yet you don't know what you really want to do with your life. I figure three areas of study should give you some options, but then again maybe it's not enough and you should try every department before you decide what you really want to do."

Liz gave him a dirty look for his sarcasm and then Rick replied again. "Oh, wait, as a college student you do get to do that. It's called general education requirements, designed to make you a more well rounded individual, or perhaps it's just called junior college, or perhaps even high school."

Liz sarcastically replied to Rick "Not all of us can be a philosophical piano player slash bartender who has it all figured out when it comes to the meaning of life. And certainly not all of us can have the talent of using what few lines we actually remembered from philosophy 101 to hit on people in a bar."

"I may be philosophical, but even I can concede that I don't have it all figured out when it comes to the meaning of life. I think Monty Python has the answers to that more than I do, but I do know that a little philosophy is a good tool to use when hitting on women Rick said with a big sarcastic smile. "See, it works because you did come. So what are your degrees in?"

Liz replied back. "My first degree is in Business and Marketing which is the one my father said I had to get if he was going to pay for my education. He made this deal with me when I was 16. I could go to any school I wanted to for my college education and he would pay for it, but I had to study business. He also told me that I could study anything else I wanted to as well, but I had to get a degree in business first. So I did my course study in business first and got done with it in three years. The other two degrees are in Astronomy and Art. I've always loved Art and really didn't want to study anything else ever since I was a kid. That is where my main passion is, but it's hard to be successful in that area unless you're a Picasso and dead. I had a roommate who got me interested in the stars so I studied Astronomy as well until I realized last year that I actually had enough credits for a degree in Astronomy."

All Rick could do was give her a weird look, mostly of shock and minor annoyance at her quirky method of storytelling. The he asked her "So are you going to actually do anything with your art degree since art is your passion, or are you doomed to work for your father's company?"

"As far as I am concerned, I'm not doomed to work for my father; the business degree was just an easy compromise so I could study what I wanted." Liz responded with a harshness in her tone because she was talking about her father. "I've applied to some art schools in Paris that I think would be really fun to study at, and if you're going to do any graduate work in Art there's probably not any better schools to do it in, so we'll see if that works out. The great thing about these schools is that there are scholarships that I could get so my father doesn't have to pay for it, and therefore he couldn't tell me that I'm wasting my time."

Rick smiled at her and refilled her coffee. He said "Well there is still hope for you even if you don't get to go to Paris. You did discover this place, and no matter if you keep coming back or not, you'll always find something to laugh at even if it's the most mindless conversation you've ever heard. All I can tell you is that there is something magical about a place like this, and it's the people in it that give it its character. I'm sure your friends from last night would disagree, but people with no sense of humor usually do."

Bud came walking out of the office after having finished counting the money and doing the daily paperwork for the bar. He looked at Rick and Liz shaking his head at Rick sense of flirtation. Bud always saw it as a flirtation with disaster when it came to Rick and women because in his mind nothing good could ever come from love even though he was happy with his marriage. This was Bud's ironic sense of humor when it came to the people he loved the most. Nobody could really explain it, but it had some comical points. He replied to Rick as he was walking out of the club. ""Don't forget to lock up tonight Romeo, and I don't want to be cleaning any disgusting messes on top of my bar from things going too far between you two."

"Hey I'm not Susan," Rick said back to Bud. "I can control who I have sex with and where I do it. But if anything does happen we'll just make her clean it up just to get her back for the last time."

"How about nothing happening so my bar keeps clean and sanitary? I don't know why you young kids just can't get a bed or wait to find a room somewhere. If there's a sign that says bar…doesn't mean have sex here."

"Apparently it does in Susan's book, but hey we love her anyway and that's only because the Bible says we have to. I know you love her as if she was your own daughter, but you have to make her clean up her own messes. I mean, you would make me clean my mess wouldn't you?"

"Don't start with me Rick; I'm not worried about her tonight as long she shows up to work tomorrow. It's you I'm not too sure about because after all, you're the piano player."

As Bud walked out of the club Rick and Liz both started laughing at his comments. Rick looked at Liz and replied to her. "Nobody trusts the piano player anymore, especially since we're the one person in a bar you should trust."

"You're also a bartender, so you do have that going against you. So what happened with Susan?"

She closed up one night and her two week boyfriend at the time stopped by to see her while she was cleaning up. Well, one thing lead to another, and she left a bigger mess than the one she was cleaning up, and most of it was on top of the bar. Bud wasn't too happy when he discovered it, and ever since that incident whoever she's dating is not allowed here at the bar after hours."

"I can see why he would be mad, but what about you? Is there reason for him to be suspicious of you?"

"I don't really know what he means by that; he's probably just getting paranoid in his old age. Besides, I'm completely innocent" Rick said with a big sarcastic smile on his face.

Liz laughed at Rick and replied "Somehow I doubt that. Every piano player I've ever met has had some skeletons in their closet. And I really doubt that there is any innocence behind you having me stay behind tonight to have a cup of coffee with you while you clean up."

"Ah, you have foiled my secret plan because after all *do you want to have a cup of coffee* with me really means *do you want to have sex with me.*

"Thank you for proving my point and I didn't know that about *'do you want to have a cup of coffee with me,'* but maybe that's only in this bar."

"Perhaps, but if that's true and you don't ever come here again, then it will mean you don't like having sex, and I don't know anybody who hates sex."

"Maybe I just don't want to have sex with anybody in this bar. Chicago is a big place and there are lots of other bars where I might find someone I like."

Rick just stared at her for a moment with a smile. He replied. "No, I'm going with my answer on this one because there has to be at least one person that you want to have sex with in this bar; it probably won't be any of my friends, but there is someone in here that you would like. Oh, and by the way, you don't have to worry about anything. My innocence will get thrown right out the door if I ask you out for breakfast tonight."

Liz smiled and then gave Rick a curious look and said to him. "Why don't we just start with dinner tomorrow before we get into the whole breakfast issue; I don't know if I can completely trust you yet."

"Hey, I told you, you can always trust the piano player. But needless to say, this is going to get interesting don't you think?"

"You're right, this is going to get interesting, but I still don't trust you yet."

"Hey, where's the faith? I mean, come on, this is not the best way to start getting to know somebody."

Liz shook her finger at Rick and smiled. Then she said. "You're pretty perceptive if you already knew what I was going to ask or what I was thinking, but in response to 'Where's my faith' have you seen any of the guys around here? Some of them are your friends!"

"Yes some of them are my friends," Rick responded. "And because of that I look a whole lot better. So I guess I'll meet you here at eight and we'll see how interesting this can really get."

Liz just smiled at Rick again and then winked at him. She was already a little infatuated with him and she knew there was something about him that could make her knees "buckle." Rick knew the same about her. After they stared at each other for a moment Liz said. "Okay tomorrow at eight then."

4

The Thing about People

It was a month later since Rick and Liz had met each other that night at the club. They were now dating and doing all the usual things that beginning couples did. They talked to each other every night sometimes falling asleep to the sound of each other's voice on the other end of the phone. They rarely spent any free time away from each other while introducing the each other to their everyday lives. Liz would see Rick at the club almost every night quickly becoming one of the regulars at *The Blue's Note* and he would help her out with school projects becoming an integral part of her life. They talked, they laughed, and the opened up a part of their lives to the other.

Sure after only a month of knowing each other they had their doubts about what good could come out of knowing each other on a intimate level. However, they felt good about seeing each other intimately, for some reason they both knew that it felt right and it made sense. So they continued, traveling a road that might not have been traveled often and hoping that it would make the best difference in their lives.

It was a Tuesday afternoon at the cub and Rick was getting the bar ready for the evening shift before he would play his usual song of the night, it was his own brand of music for life. Chad and Charlie were there as well waiting for the third member of their Tuesday domino game. They were waiting on the Judge.

His name was Judge George McClain and he was a municipal court judge from the neighborhood who had known Chad and Charlie as since they were children. Their mother Janet was his court clerk for over twenty years and the judge took to looking after the boys since they didn't have a father in their lives. It was a strange relationship he had with them since they were sort of criminals and he was a man of the law, but he had hope for them.

He couldn't very well put them in jail when they were in his court for violating some misdemeanor charge because he had promised their mother when she died that he would look out for her boys. Putting them in jail no matter how much they deserved it would have broken that promise. So as a strange and ironic consolation he played dominos with Chad and Charlie every Tuesday so he could look in after them and try to influence them on living a good life.

The Judge as everybody called him was another one of those happy go lucky characters from the neighborhood that one couldn't help but like. He also knew everybody and he had known Rick for a long time just like Chad and Charlie. The Judge on a number of occasions while Rick was growing up had tried to get Rick out of a household with and Alcoholic mother, but had always been unsuccessful due to glitches in the legal system. Rick just became another one of those unfortunate souls that he would look after and become good friends with. The Judge was a regular at *The Blue's Note* and had been coming since Rick first started playing years ago when he was growing up.

The Judge came strolling in the clubs with his usual carefree look on his face and smiled at everyone that was there. Rick said to him as he came walking towards the bar to get a beer "Hey judge, how are you doing today?"

The Judge replied back. "I'm old and one more day closer to death, so you can imagine the mood I'm in today. By the way, I hear you have a new love in your life and you've been seeing her for more than two weeks this time."

Rick gave Chad and Charlie a dirty look as he responded to the Judge. "I didn't know that my love life had reached the inner sanctums of the municipal court. I wonder who I have to thank for that one."

The Judge said to Rick. "Actually my bailiff told me this time. Apparently, he met her not too long ago in here, but it was Chad who dispensed with all the details."

Chad shrugged his shoulders and had a look on his face that said he didn't do anything. The he gave Rick a sarcastic innocent look and said "All I told him was that you were seeing someone again and you were happy."

Rick smiled at him satirically while he paused for a moment at Chad's explanation. He responded to his friend. "But how much did you embellish in your tale? That's what I'm worried about."

Rick looked around at everybody as they were going about their business and said to everyone in the bar " I wish everybody around here would quit thinking of me as the Sam Malone of the bar. I just happen to know most of the women that come in here and occasionally I ask one of them out."

The Charlie with a chuckle in his voice replied to Rick ""Yeah, but how well you know all of them is the point we're making."

"Those are just mere rumors and you have no proof of anything. That's the story I am sticking to." Rick said in a sarcastic tone

The judge sat down with his beer to play dominos with Chad and Charlie. He was shaking his head at the three boys and their playful insulting of one another just like brothers often did. He was laughing to himself while shaking his head because the way the three of them were around each other hadn't changed in the twenty years he had known them. It was familiar and as the Judge often said when one got older it was best to stick with what was familiar for it was the only thing comforting when you were heading towards dying days. *The Blue's Note* was familiar because of the people in it and for a man who never had any children of his own or a huge family o go home the people and the place became an instant comfort.

The Judge looked at Chad and Charlie and said. "Are you two ready for me to kick your ass in dominos? If you two let me win this time, the next time I find you in my court I'll actually throw you in jail instead of just making you pay a fine."

Charlie replied back to the Judge. "We never let you win. You're really that good at dominos, and we wouldn't just say that to make an old man feel good."

"Or is it to make me go easy on you every time you end up in my court. Don't patronize me. I know you two professional criminals are better at these kinds of games than you let on. Remember, I'm a judge. I see criminals every day, and I know how you think."

Chad playfully responded. "Now judge, you know I'm not that good at dominos. Checkers is my game, but there isn't any money in it."

Rick was laughing at this point, he was laughing at his two friends continually trying to swindle the one guy who could put them in jail. He simply replied with a laugh "Judge, don't let him fool you. The game he's really good at is gay chicken. I've never seen anybody play it better."

The Judge stared at Chad with a bewildered look for he didn't know what kind of game they were talking about, but it sounded bad in his mind. Before he could say anything Chad interjected and said. "Come on, Rick. You know I've only won one game, but it doesn't mean anything. The guy I beat didn't even know what the game was, so that was the only reason I won."

The Judge looked around the room and finally replied "What in the hell is gay chicken. Is that some weird sex game that you young people are into now because it sounds disgusting to me."

Rick said."Gay chicken is where someone dares you to try and kiss another guy, and just like an old fashioned game of chicken, whoever breaks first is the loser, but as the winner it isn't saying much if you're straight.; Oh, and Chad is the only one who lost to a real gay man who thought he was trying to hit on him."

Everybody started laughing as Chad was getting angry. The Judge asked Chad "Is this true Chad? Are you trying to tell us something about yourself, because you don't need to hide in a closet all your life! There is no judgment on our part if your lifestyle is a little bit different than everybody else's. Your mother would be disappointed in you, of course, but *we* wouldn't judge… no pun intended."

Chad stood up out of his chair and replied "I want everybody to know for the last time I am not gay, and I can't believe you would actually think that about me. Can't anybody see how much I love women, even though I have no success with them and they don't understand me?"

Chad sat at the table to play dominoes with an angry look upon his face as everybody starts to laugh. Liz walked into the club and headed for the bar to give Rick a kiss. The room seemed to light up as she walked in and she is greeted by everyone. There wasn't anybody in the bar that wasn't glad to see her as she was received by smiles and warm welcomes. Even Old Man Henderson was delighted to see her as he gives her a wink.

In the month since she first started to come to the club and started dating Rick she has been received as one of the regulars. She has struck a great friendship with everybody quickly and they became forever changed by her. Liz just had that way with people and she was already seen as the best thing for Rick. After giving Rick a kiss she said to everyone "Hey guys, how's everybody doing today?" She looked at Chad and then back at Rick and asked "What's wrong with him?"

"Oh he's mad because we told the judge here about the game that he's really, really good at."

"Oh, you mean gay chicken?"

Everybody started laughing as Liz gave a sarcastic smile to Chad. The Judge gave everybody a dirty look for making fun of Chad, but he was someone that could take delighting the razzing of Chad since he had know him for so long and he often had to get him out of trouble.

Chad said to everybody. "You guys are *not* funny; I think every one of you are trying to start rumors because you think it's funny."

Charlie gave his brother a big smile and said to him. "Actually, it is pretty funny whether it's a rumor or not. It's funny because even though it's not a big deal, you get mad at everybody anyway for thinking you're gay."

Rick smiled at his friends and walked around the bar to introduce Liz to the Judge. Rick said. "Liz, I haven't introduced you to the judge yet; he's one of our regulars from the neighborhood. He hasn't been in for awhile, so you haven't had a chance to meet." Pointing at the Judge he said. "Liz, this is the judge. Judge this is Liz, the woman I've been dating."

Liz smiled at him and stuck out her hand to offer a hand shake and replied "It's nice to meet you. The Judge looked at her with a curious eye and then looked her up and down. He was getting a good look at her trying to see what Rick liked about her, but more importantly he was seeing if there was something about her, more than just a pretty face.

He finally responded to her "It's nice to finally meet the person that I keep hearing is making Rick so happy. I can see why he likes you."

Liz had a strange look on her face because of the Judge's comment. Then she responded. "I don't think I quite understand the basis of approval, but I guess I should consider it a compliment."

The Judge looked at her with a cock eyes smile and replied "You can say that; I've known Rick for a long time, and I also know what kind of woman it will take to make him fall again, so I just wanted to see if you fit the bill."

Liz looked at him with a curious look and replied back "What do you mean make Rick fall again?"

Before the Judge could say anything Rick interjected. He said to Liz. "Look, before the rumors of my past love life come out and you start adding to those rumors, why don't you get back to your game and I'll see about getting you a free drink?"

She looked a little confused about how Rick was acting. The judge gave the okay sign to Rick and smiled at Liz which made her even more confused. She shook her head at all secrecy and then said. "Rick, I came by to tell you that I can't make it tonight. I have to help out at the concert tonight on campus. A friend of mine said she needed some help at the last minute so I said yes."

"Don't worry about it," he replied. "We'll do it again some other time. By the way, who's in concert tonight?"

She looked at him with a weird look not realizing that they would know who the singer was. Liz replied. "It's a blues singer who's apparently from Chicago. His name is Lee Wayne Johnson, but I've never heard of him before. He went to De Paul years ago, so he's doing a concert there tonight."

Everybody looked at her with surprise and excitement. Chad was the first speak and he replied "Wait a minute, there's a Lee Wayne Johnson concert tonight at the University?"

"You've heard of him" Liz replied

Rick laughed a bit and responded. "Yeah, we all know him because he grew up in the neighborhood, and he also used to play here before he made it big. I actually got to jam with him a few times here when I was in high school. He's now a famous blues artist along the same lines as Stevie Ray Vaughn."

"Well that's good, because I had some extra tickets for all of you." She replied.

Charlie had a huge sarcastic smile on his face and then he replied to Liz "Just how many tickets did you get girlfriend, if you don't mind me asking? "

Chad followed his brother's lead and responded "Yeah, because if you have any extra tickets you don't need, we can sure use them." Liz pulled the tickets out of her purse and replied "I only have four, so you boys will have to divide them amongst yourselves"

Rick grabbed them before Chad and Charlie could get a hold of them. He thanked Liz by kissing her and then he replied. "Now if I give you two tickets, then you can't scalp them. The fourth one is for Bud."

Chad gave Rick his best innocent look "Hey, what do you take us for? We actually want to go to this concert! And not everything we do is about making money either."

Charlie looked at Rick with a sympathetic look and said. "My poor pathetic excuse for a brother is actually right. We're not the materialistic weasels that you think we are; we don't always think about money."

The Judge shook his head and cleared his throat to remind Chad and Charlie that they had been in his court many times for scalping tickets and other criminal activities. They both looked at the judge with a dirty look as he was examining his dominos for his next play.

Rick gave them a serious look and replied. "I mean it guys, don't be scalping tickets at the university. The last time you got caught there, I stuck up for you and nearly lost my scholarship. If you get caught again I'm not bailing you two out of jail."

Charlie with a sarcastic tone said. "After all these years Rick, I thought you would have thought better of us. I guess I was wrong about you."

Rick said. "No, it's because I know you too well." He yelled back towards the office "Bud, come out here for a minute."

Bud came waling out of the office and said "What is it Rick? I'm actually trying to do some work."

"Liz got us tickets to the Lee Wayne Johnson concert and there's one for you."

"Lee Wayne Johnson is playing in concert? Sure I love to see a local boy play in concert. It's definitely been a while since we've seen him. Where's he playing tonight?"

"He's playing at the university, one night only."

Bud laughed to himself and walked back towards the office, as he was walking he responded. "I guess we're closing early tonight, but hell, it's worth it to see that boy."

Liz said to Rick. "So I guess I'll see you there?"

He looked at her with a big smile and replied "You can count on it, and since you got us the tickets I guess I'll have to be nice and take you to one of my favorite places on campus."

She laughed and replied back. "It's not one of those kinky places I'm always hearing about, is it? If it is, then you're getting a little too presumptuous when it comes to properly thanking me for the tickets."

"You really have to quit listening to rumors about me in this bar." He said to her in a sarcastic tone.

Liz kissed him goodbye and said. "I'll see you tonight."

Rick smiled at her and kissed her again. She turned around and said goodbye to everybody then walked out. Rick was smiling as she left, happy to feel in love as he once did. After she left he looked over and saw everybody staring at him. They all had sarcastic smiles on their face and then Rick asked. "What. What did I do?"

Chad was the first to speak up and he replied "So I think we might be hearing the chiming of wedding bells."

Rick gave him a dirty look and replied back "Shut up, this isn't high school. I don't even want to think about that evil institution."

"No, he's just think about the making whoopee part and then going right into the pitter patter of little feet."

Before Rick could respond Chad said. "Hey you're right. That's the Rick we know, going straight from the little sin into the big sin. Only Rick would be thinking about showing her the night of her young fertile life." Rick responded in kind "And those are the only details you will ever know. What I show her is my business."

The Judge looked at all of them with a dirty look and replied. "I thought you were good catholic boys, didn't you learn anything about how to avoid sin in catholic school?"

Rick, Chad, and Charlie looked at the judge with serious looks. They all answered at the same time "No."

∞∞∞∞∞∞∞∞

Later that night Rick and Bud were standing outside the theater at the end of the concert waiting for Chad and Charlie. Rick is also waiting for Liz to finish helping her friend at the box office. They had enjoyed the concert, but shortly after it started Chad and Charlie disappeared. They were up to no good as usual and Rick knew it. He could tell them every time not to do any criminal activities, but somehow they would find a way to get into trouble. Rick and Bud just stood there waiting.

Bud finally spoke up and said. "Where are those SOB'S? If they're in trouble again and got arrested then I'm definitely not bailing them out this time."

Rick said."Who knows where they went this time? I should've known that as soon as we got here they would disappear and probably start doing something illegal. Sometimes they're just like children who never listen."

Bud grumbled and replied to Rick. "Well, I'm not waiting for them anymore, and if you see them tell 'em they owe me breakfast just like they promised."

"How many times have they really lived up to their promises? Hey, they're my friends, but let's be honest here."

"You're right, and I don't know why I give them the benefit of the doubt, but we'll see how they like it when they can't get free beer anymore. Anyway, I'm off."

"I'll see you tomorrow." Rick said to his old friend.

Bud walked off and started home as the crowd from the concert was dispersing. Liz finally came
walking up to Rick as he was standing there in front of the Concert hall.
Liz asked "Well how was it, were the tickets pretty close?"

Rick replied back "Yeah, you certainly out did yourself with these tickets, which means that I'm going to have to be really nice to you for awhile."

She laughed and said to Rick. "Oh, you're going to have to be more than just nice; something along the lines of being treated like a queen comes to mind."

"Yeah, you're not much different than any other woman I've met."

"Probably, but I'm more fun. So was Lee Wayne Johnson just as good as you remember him when he played the club?"

"Yeah, he still has the stuff. Say, you want to meet him? After all, I might as well use this back stage pass you gave me."

"Sure, I've never met a real blues musician before and it will be nice to see what he has to say about you since you two know each other."

Rick just smiled at her with his famous knowing smile as they walked back inside the auditorium. It was a smile showing her how happy he was with heart that moment. He wanted her to know him as well as the musicians he played with knew him.

You see, musicians were like fortune tellers in a way they know true essence of someone by the notes they play. Lee Wayne Johnson would never have to hold a conversation with Rick in order to know who he really was; he would know because they had once played together. Rick would always just like his mentor Gus would tell him that was an instinctive thing between artists much like breathing a slow paced tempo to calm the senses.

Liz and Rick walk back stage to where the dressing rooms where to see Lee Wayne Johnson. They had back stage passes so they were let though without any hassle unlike many members of the audience who were trying to squeeze through, most of whom were female. Liz was a little surprised to see so many women trying to get back stage to see Lee; he wasn't that good looking she thought, but she also didn't know the power of the music scene in Chicago especially when it came to the blues. Lee was talking to some older musicians when out of the corner of his eye he saw Rick.

He quickly shook hands with the people he was talking to and rushed over to Rick. Lee replied to him "Hey Rick, haven't seen you in a long time. What are you doing here?"

Rick shook his hand and responded back "Well I heard you were in Town and I was given some free tickets to your concert. I thought I better come out and see if you've actually developed any talent"

Lee said with a sarcastic laugh "What, are you saying I'm not good enough to for you to buy tickets to see my show? "

Rick smiled and replied "Do you really want me to answer that? Hey, if I can get free tickets to something I'm definitely there being the struggling musician and all."

"I see why you really came to my concert. So what are you doing these days" Lee asked Rick?

"I'm still playing at *The Blue's Note* and helping Bud with the place."
"So how is Bud? I bet he hasn't changed a bit."

Well he still isn't dead, and he's still grouchy as ever. I'm sure that will never change."

"I'd say you're right about that. So I guess you're still doing what you love the most, uh?"

"That's right, couldn't imagine anything better. By the way, this is Liz, she's a student here and she's actually the one who got the tickets for me" Rick replied back to Lee point in the direction of Liz.

Lee smiled at Rick's comment and then looked at Liz. He stared at her taking in all her beauty and then winked at her replying "Don't you know this guy has to be charged double when he comes to my concert? If he's told you any bad things about me from my club days, then I'll go ahead and tell you that they're all true except for my musical ability; despite him, I actually have some."

Liz smile at him and began to laugh. Before she could say anything Rick responded "This guy is the main reason there are a lot of rumors about me at the club. After all, you know how those blues artists can be, just a lot of made up stories about other people's pain and stupid mistakes."

Liz budded in and replied. "If your theory is correct then I really can't trust anything you've said to me so far. Is trying to show off in front of a music star your way of showing your manhood or will you just measure your instruments to show off your manhood?"

Both Rick and Lee paused for a moment to give a Liz a dirty look then they started laughing. Lee said to Rick "You know its love when she can put you in place while showing off in front of you friends and then have you figured out to a tee. Just for putting him in his place, you're always welcome at any one of my concerts as one of my personal guests."

Rick couldn't help but laugh because there was a little bit of truth in what Lee said.

He smiled even more at Liz because she wasn't afraid to let out her feisty side. Although her shyness was sweet and made her beautiful, it was her feistiness that made her attractive and enduring. It was the start of him falling in love with her and even though he would not admit it out loud it was time to admit it to himself.

Rick looked back over at Lee and said "The concert was great. If you're still around tomorrow you should stop by the club and have a beer on us. I think I should get out of here before Liz really shows me up."

Liz said "You know you like it.

Rick smiled and said. "Sure, we can say that if it makes you feel better."

"That's not what you were saying last night" Liz responded.

Rick gave her a weird look as her feistiness was getting worse. He thought to himself that she might be drunk, but he knew her better than that. She just had a playful side that made her sexy in some strange way that he couldn't describe in words. He finally laughed and shook his head at her.

Lee said. "Not even Linda could make you have that kind of look; it definitely must be love for you."

Liz was taken by surprise with the comment made by Lee. She had heard bits and pieces about Linda, Rick's ex-girlfriend for whom he was very serious with. However she still didn't know what had happened with them and it occurred to her that there was still a lot about Rick she didn't know. One of the more important things she didn't know was how easily it was to break his heart and what he would be like after it happened

Rick laughed again at Lee's comment then he extended his hand to shake Lee's He replied to Lee "She's something isn't she? It was good to see you again, but I'm going to get out of here before any more bad memories come rushing to the surface."

"It was good to see you; and Liz, it was very nice to meet you." Lee replied.

Liz said to Lee as she shook his hand. "It was very nice to meet you and I'll try not to give in to his bullshit. So thank you for warning me about him."

"Anytime."

Rick looked at the both of them with a big smile and said. "We better leave before my so called bad reputation gets any bigger."

As they walked out of the building Liz was giving Rick an interesting look. It wasn't that she was mad, just curious about Rick and his past. She realized how much she didn't know, but she wasn't sure how much she wanted to know. Rick wasn't sure how much he wanted to tell her, but they both knew that they couldn't make anything work between them if they hid behind the mask of silent dishonesty. They both knew at that moment that cared for each other so they had to dispense with their little secrets. The haunting truth for Rick at the moment was he would have to tell her about Linda and how she broke his heart.

5

The Home of Old Friends

Rick and Liz walked around the De Paul campus for a while talking and telling interesting stories about their college days. Rick had lots of stories to tell her and all of them like most college stories ended with some embarrassing moment that nobody wanted to remember, but was too funny not to tell someone. Liz realized that there was a bit of rebellious side in Rick; it was his lust for life and his satirical outlook on things from working in a dingy blues club could bring out. What Liz didn't understand was that there was certain way of looking at things Rick had learned over the years that came from his harsh years of experience. She didn't understand because she had never gone through anything tragic yet.

They made their way to the very center of campus. All that was there among the oak trees and long extended sidewalks that led into the old weathered brick buildings was a park bench. It was a single park bench that seemed to be out of place, but in a strange twist of ironic fate it was in the perfect place. Liz looked at Rick funny and said, "This is your favorite spot on campus, uh. It's a park bench."

Rick smiled at her and replied. "Yes, this is it. It's simple, right in the center of things on the campus. There's no mystery behind my favorite spot if that's what you're looking for. What can I say I like the simple life!"

"I was looking for something a little more kinky since I've heard all these interesting things about you."

Rick just laughed and said. "They're just stories; it doesn't mean that they're true. Although, if you have your doubts, then I guess you'll just have to find out yourself"

"I can just imagine what you have in mind, which brings up the subject."

"I don't need a subject, I need a good imagination.".

Liz continued with her dirty look towards Rick, She said."I'm sure you do, but that has nothing to do with what I really want to know I want to know what Lee Wayne Johnson meant by Linda couldn't even do that to you. I'm not one to ask about past lovers, but I'm curious about what effect she had on you to make you be the way you are.

Rick sat back on bench and paused in deep thought at the question. It was a loaded question, the kind that's never an easy answer. He looked at her with a serious look and said. "I think anybody you love when they're gone affects you in some profound way, and if you want to know the truth, yes she had an effect on me, especially when she left."

Liz looked at her with a concerned look and replied "Well you haven't talked about what happened with you and her or why you've come to believe what you believe. I want to know what happened."

"Do you really want to know, or do you just want to know if the rumors you've heard about me are really true."

"I don't care about the rumors, I'm just curious about her and how you got to this point in your life" She replied back.

Rick thought for a moment while looking deep inside her. Although it didn't make much sense, he was looking beyond her pretty face and beautiful smile-he was looking into her soul. He finally replied. "Okay I'll tell you, but you have to tell me about your ex as well, and I do have a serious question for you."

Liz thought for a moment and with a smile on her face said. "Okay, but I'll let you ask yours first."

"That' so nice of you. I am curious though, why have you waited so long to ask this? I would've thought that this is something you would have asked me a couple of weeks ago."

"I wanted to get to know you a little bit better before I asked you this kind of question. You told me a little the second time I talked to you, but I think there's a certain point in relationships when you can ask these kinds of serious questions."

Rick responded with a little sarcasm "See, that just proves my theory about people; when you start out dating you should just hand out a dating resume to each other so you don't have to wait to get certain questions answered. The dating resume could have things like: I dated this many people, been in love this many times, these women have had this kind of effect on me, and just for added bonus to bypass the really embarrassing question that we all want to ask, but are too afraid because of the answer, how many people have you had sex with?"

Liz nodded and smiled while laughing bit at his theory then said. "You're right that would probably help, but it would take all the fun out of having these kinds of conversations on a park bench with such a romantic setting. You never know what might happen in a place like this."

"I knew you were a tease, but most women are and I should know because I am a bartender/piano player. We do know a lot and we do see how women can really be."

"And I'm sure the alcohol in your place has no effect whatsoever on how women act. But enough of being a sexist, please just answer my question."

Rick laughed and responded back to her. "You don't really want to hear about ex girlfriends? I mean, somehow it just seems wrong to talk about an ex. You know that no matter what I say you won't like it because you'll think I'm just comparing you to her."

She laughed at his satirical way of dodging questions. He was trying to pull off some type of Humphrey Bogart quality, but it wasn't working on her. She said to him. Quit stalling and just tell me; I'll decide if I want to get mad or not."

Rick smiled back at her replying. "Okay," then he leaned back on the park bench and began to tell his story.

He explained to her that the reason that everybody knew about Linda was that she had grown up with him. She was from the same neighborhood as Rick, Chad, and Charlie. Her parents were hardworking middle class parents just like everybody else trying to provide a better life for their children. Linda went to the same catholic school as Rick ever since they were in elementary school and for Rick was the only boy she ever liked in school. She caught his eye very early on and when he figured out that girls were not that gross she was the one he like the most. As they grew up together they were rarely apart from one another.

They also had one common thread between them, they both had alcoholic parents. Her father was an alcoholic and when Linda needed to escape her dismal abusive household she would run away to Rick's. They would escape there dismal lives together, always together, and it wasn't long that the connection between them was formed. Linda and Rick were childhood and highs school sweethearts; they seemed to be that fairy tale true love that people were always looking to find. Everybody who knew Rick knew her as well; Rick and Lind were looked at as always being together, forever just like how true love should be. Linda was the one that knew Rick better than anybody and he knew her just the same.

Liz felt like Rick was stalling a little bit as he told this story, but in order to tell her the whole story and make her understand he had to tell it from the beginning. She just smiled as he continued and he smiled back at her as he continued his narrative. He knew what she was thinking, but he was going to tell her the truth, the whole ugly truth.

Rick said to her. "You noticed that, did you? Maybe I'm kind of skirting the issue, but the truth is I haven't talked about this in a very long time." He paused for a moment as Liz gave him a small sympathetic smile then Rick started to tell his story.

Rick was very much in love with Linda and she in no small way had a tremendous affect on me. It felt in a lot of ways that Rick was defined by her when they were a couple and she changed his life in a profound way. Rick wasn't stupid, He knew that a person couldn't make you who you are, but for him Linda came pretty damn close.

She was there when he needed her the most. She was there after his mother died more than anyone could be. Linda could do the best thing in the world Rick, she could make him laugh. Linda also never seemed to mind that the neighborhood they grew up in was home and Rick didn't want to leave. It was all of these things that made Rick love her

Although Rick would later find out the hard way that the last part was more of a delusion. Truth is, the hardest thing about her leaving was finding out that she didn't want to stay in the place that they had called home. Rick thought for a moment that, it probably didn't make any sense, but it was the simple truth.

Rick smile at her and said. "So there's my one piece of honesty for the evening. Now, what's your story? I want to know about this former love of your life since I've told you all about mine."

Liz smiled and replied. "I guess it's only fair that I tell you about my ex since you've been honest with me. But I do think that this is the last time we should talk about ex lovers, and for your information, I'm not worried about being compared to Linda...what do you think; no more talk about former lovers?"

Rick said. "That's music to my ears! Besides, we shouldn't have to be those sad and pathetic souls who dwell on the past and usually sit in my bar night after night nursing their regrets with a stiff drink."

"I'd like to think that were better people than that, but like Charlie said once, sometimes our delusions get the best of us" Liz said

"But sometimes our delusions tend to be better than our own reality, and if that's the case, no one can really judge us when it comes to our delusions. Now you quit stalling and tell me about this ex lover of yours."

Liz started telling her story. "If you must know, I met him my first year of college and he was a few years older than me. We really didn't have anything in common, but I had love in my eyes when I first saw him so I immediately became infatuated with him.

When you're looking hard for love, even the wrong person will seem right. He was smart and funny and knew all about the world, but most importantly my father didn't approve, so it made the relationship even better on some level."

"So you're saying that you're not different than other young girls in wanting to piss your father off with dating men that he will never approve of."

Liz smiled at his comment and responded "No, not really, and when I was eighteen and nineteen I was hell bent on making my father mad at anything I did. The thing is, I really did like Scott and I think with him I learned how to love. He graduated and moved to New York so he could pursue a career in politics. He would call and send letters, but they became less and less. After a while I never heard from him again, and then I heard he got married. My story isn't very original, but that's what happened. My father on the other hand was very glad he left, and proceeded to tell me a very big *I told you so.*"

Rick gave her a serious look, something he hadn't done all night long. "I would venture a guess that your father really didn't like Scott because he was a Democrat, and your father, being a lifelong Republican, just couldn't have a Democrat spreading his demon seed upon his daughter."

Liz smiled and said. "That was the main reason why he hated Scott, but the truth is that my father is just a big asshole and doesn't like anybody who isn't the mirror image of him, especially when it comes to his kind of politics."

"Ah, one of those. I can tell your dad and I will be the best of friends"

"Well I don't know how well Jesus and the anti-Christ would get along before things came to blows, but I'm pretty sure it would be something like that with you and my dad."

"Perhaps, but I like to think that I can be the better person and not just deliberately make your dad angry."
"I'm sure it wouldn't be that at all. My dad would just hate you on general principle because he's an asshole."

"You really don't like your dad that much do you; why is that?"

Liz paused for a moment and then replied to Rick. "I love my dad, but at the same time I hate him and it's because he doesn't see me for who I am. He doesn't understand me and I think he never has. He only sees me for what he wants me to be; and yes if you are wondering there are a lot of things I do just to make him mad. My college education is partly based on that as well."

"As well as some of your choices in your love life?"

"Sure, but I'm no different than a lot of people in life."

Rick looked away from her for a moment and gathered a thought. Then he said. Isn't it funny how finding that true love of our life is sometimes paralleled to making someone else mad, whether it's through jealousy or parental revenge or even just in spite? Can you imagine a person shouting to the moon 'well I'll show so and so' and spend the rest of my life with someone that doesn't make me happy just to get back at them? And you know that the other person doesn't even care what you do to try and get back at them for something that they didn't quite realize made you mad to begin with."

Liz responded in kind to Rick. "I think you have a good point, but I think you have also engaged in too many stupid philosophical conversations at the bar with Chad and Charlie to be making those types of impressions. There comes a time when your little conversations get the best of you and you start going off on some authoritative tangent that doesn't make sense."

"I thought you said I had a good point?"

"I did, but sometimes you take it a little too far and then start sounding like a Baptist preacher on Sunday."

"I never realized I did that with my little philosophical speeches; you're really beginning to sound like my..."

Liz cut him off before he could finish that sentence and said, "Your wife or perhaps someone that is beginning to know you very well?"

Rick said. "Yeah, I'm getting a little scared now. This thing between us is not going to work if I don't have some kind of mystery left."

Liz smiled at him and replied back. "you still have some mystery left, although not as much as you think, but I still want you to tell me more about yourself. When it comes to people I want to know well, I have to figure out if it's worth it. What can I say, like you I try to be a good judge of people and that comes from paying attention."

"Then you're learning very well and as long as I still have a little bit of mystery left, then all of my charm is not wasted on you" Rick said to her.

Liz smiled at Rick again and replied "I don't think you'll ever have to worry about that; after all, I'm still here."

Rick said to her in a serious tone "Yes you are," then he leaned in to give Liz a kiss. She welcomed the kiss and it brought a sense of joy that she had never felt. As they were kissing they heard someone running behind them and became startled. The stopped kissing abruptly as Chad and Charlie came running up to them while they were sitting on the park bench.

While out of breath Charlie said "Rick, you got to say we've been with you all night; we're being chased by the police."

"What did you do this time" Rick asked his friend.

Before Charlie could say anything Chad responded. "They caught us scalping tickets, but we were able to get away before they saw who we were. Two cops have been chasing us half way through campus."

Rick replied back in anger "Didn't I tell you not to scalp your tickets? I told you that you would get caught here on campus. I'm so tired of covering for you guys."

"Come on dude, just say that we've been here with you all night, the police are going to be here any second and you know we would do it for you." Chad replied back

Rick responded in a sarcastic tone. "I wouldn't be stupid enough to do something like this so I could get caught for wrong doing."

Chad started to speak up but Liz cut him and replied "Rick, leave them alone; we'll just say that they've been here with us all evening."

"Yeah Rick, just cover for us or we'll have to call you again for bail money" Chad said.

Rick cursed under his breath and shook his fist at Chad then said "Your bail fund is empty, and I'm tired of covering for you. You should..."

Before Rick could finish his sentence the two police officers that had been chasing Chad and Charlie across campus finally showed up at the park bench that everybody was at. The first officer replied pointing at Chad and Charlie "You two are under arrest."

"Officer, what did these two men do" Rick asked the police officer.

The second officer said to Rick "They were scalping tickets at the concert and when we tried to arrest them they resisted arrest by running away."

"These two! They can't be the same men you're looking for because they've been here all night with me and her" Rick said.

The first officer replied "We saw them so don't try to lie for them." He walked over to Chad and Charlie to put his handcuffs on them and arrest them.

Rick sidestepped to get in his way and said. "I'm not lying for them. Are you sure you saw these two men, or two men or women that look like these two people."

The first officer pushed Rick out of the way and proceeded to try and arrest Chad and Charlie again. He then replied. "We saw these two scalping tickets outside the concert hall and we're not going to keep defending our actions to you."

Rick didn't know what else to do as the officer what turning Chad and Charlie around to pad them down and search them for weapon. He thought for a moment and spoke up again saying "Okay, but can you describe what they look like."

He paused for a moment to let the police officers think about it for a moment. Then responded. "You can't describe what they look like can you? I guess that's okay, but I know what judge they will appear before if you do arrest them, and he doesn't act too kindly when people are arrested under false pretenses. But hey, if you're willing to deal with that and put a black mark on what I'm sure are two fine careers in the police department, then don't let me stand in your way or tell you how to do your job."

The second officer asked Rick "And what judge do you know?"

"Judge MacLean," Rick replied. "He's a regular at the bar that I run and I've known him since I was a kid. And if you really want to know, these two characters have had this happen before. The last time this happened the police officer that did it, who was a twenty year veteran of the department, got in so much trouble he was demoted to a crossing guard for the remainder of his career. But don't take that into consideration if you don't want to."

The first officer asked. "So you know Judge MacLean?"

"Yes I do, he's a good friend of mine," Rick said. Chad said under his breath to Rick "he's your best friend," Then Rick finished his statement. "He's my best friend if you really want to know."

The first officer responded back "I don't know. You could be lying. How do I know that the only reason you know him is because you

appeared before him once and now you're just using his name to make us go away?"
Hey if you want to take that gamble then go right ahead. What if you're wrong, though" Rick replied back.

Before the police officer could respond back "Officer, there's no reason to keep going round and round like this. These two men have been with us all night. I know that because this one," pointing at Chad," is my boyfriend." And these two," pointing at Rick and Charlie "are together." We were on a double date tonight. Now do I look like someone who's going to lie to you?"

Chad gave a surprised look to Liz when she mentioned that she was his girlfriend. Rick and Charlie both just stared in disbelief at her when she said that they were a couple. Nobody thought it was funny except her, but she had to think of something to say to the police. Liz had to think fast about what to say, she was trying to convince the police officers that Chad and Charlie were with them all night and she was going to play upon the police officers homophobia. She hoped that they might not see the obvious.

The first officer replied to Liz "Well I still don't know if you're lying or not, prove to me that you're not lying."

"Okay if he wasn't my boyfriend would I be willing to do this" she replied as she leaned over and gave Chad a kiss on the lips. Rick and Charlie couldn't believe what she did and after a brief moment of disbelief Rick started to get a little mad at the whole situation. However Liz kissing Chad wasn't the biggest shocker of the evening.

The first officer said to Liz. "That doesn't mean anything. What about these two," pointing at Charlie and Rick? "If these two were going out then they would be willing to kiss each other in front of us. I want to see them do it..."

Rick and Charlie gave the police officers dirty looks while Chad began to laugh quietly. Both of the Rick and Charlie looked at Liz and started to shake their heads as if to say no, but as much as they both didn't want to do it they knew it might be the only way to convince the police officers that they were in fact a couple and that Chad and Charlie had been there all night with Rick and Liz.

Liz gave a sarcastic smile and said "I guess you boys better show your affection for each other."

The Chad in order to make fun of his brother and best friend said "Go ahead, you know you two don't mind public displays of affection."

Charlie gave his brother a very dirty look and Rick responded to the police officers "Alright we'll kiss each other if that's what you want to see."

Rick grabbed Charlie and leaned in to give him a kiss. He was trying to do his best Al Pacino impression from The Godfather Part 2 when the second police officer started to protest at them kissing one another. Charlie was a little surprised when Rick grabbed him as well as the others, but fortunately for all of them the police officers stopped them before they kissed.

The second officer replied "Alright, that's just disgusting. We don't need to see that."

The first officer also responded by saying "Okay I guess you're right, you wouldn't be a couple if you weren't willing to kiss each other, but that doesn't mean that you two," pointing at Chad and Charlie, "weren't scalping tickets and having your friends cover for you."

Rick replied to the officer. "Seriously, do these two look smart enough to scalp tickets and get away with it?"

Chad and Charlie gave Rick a dirty look because of the comment he had made about them. Liz just laughed at Rick's sarcasm; it was his way of trying to put humor into the situation. Then the first officer replied "Well, maybe you're right, but I better not catch any of you or anybody that looks like you scalping tickets."

Rick in a really sarcastic tone said. "Okay that doesn't make much sense officer, but we'll do what you say. So you have a good night now, and we'll try our best not to get into trouble."

"I don't need sarcasm out of you right now, or I'll haul you down town" the first officer replied.

Rick said to him. "Sorry Officer, it's about all I can do right now, but I don't think it's against the law, so you have a good evening."

The first officer didn't respond, he just shook his finger at Rick like a parent to a disobedient child. Then the two police officers left the park area shaking their heads and mumbling to themselves about what just happened. They didn't want to be around what they thought might some gay lover's quarrel being the open-minded individuals that they were.

Charlie just looked at Rick with a dirty look and replied to him. "We're not smart enough to get way with scalping tickets, huh? You're a real friend."

`"Hey, I'm the kind of friend that gets you out of trouble. Besides, I almost kissed you to get the police officers to leave."

"Yeah, it's enough to make me vomit and I can't believe you were actually going to kiss me."

"I had to do something to get you out of trouble, but I wasn't going to actually kiss you. I just wanted to call the cop's bluff."

"Well I think you succeeded in that; anyway I think your girlfriend here said all that needed to be said to make those cops leave. Charlie looked at Liz as he finished saying. "I can't believe you said I was gay and Rick was my lover. Do I look gay or put off that kind of vibe? "

She smiled at him and said. "Do you really want me to answer that? I wouldn't complain too much. Whatever I said was convincing enough to make the police leave and to keep you and your brother out of jail."

Charlie paused for a moment and replied "I guess that's true, but Rick being my lover is a little far-fetched. He really isn't my type and he's not that good looking."

Rick laughed a bit and responded. "That's good to know; I guess I won't have to worry about you hitting on me anymore."

"You know you love it. Hey my lame-ass brother hasn't said anything for awhile, which is unusual. What happened to you Chad? Being kissed by a real live woman put you into shock didn't it?"

"I guess Liz made quite the impression on, but then again I think any woman that actually kissed him would be the same way."

"Oh thanks," Liz replied back, that's a nice thing to say about me. I've never had any complaints before, especially out of you."

Chad started to get a little angry "Guys, leave me alone. I don't go into shock every time a woman kisses me. I just get a little nervous. I'm also a little surprised that Liz actually kissed me."

"Chad, we're all a little surprised about that" Rick replied.

Charlie looked at his brother with a funny look and replied "Chad, I'm just surprised that she was willing to make physical contact you with at all."

"You guys leave him alone, he's not that repulsive" Liz said.

Chad laughed and said. "See Charlie you were wrong, some women don't find me repulsive and just maybe they find me a little bit better looking than you.”

“Hey little brother, bullshit comes in many forms.”

“Can the three of you ever say anything nice to each other.” Liz responded with a stern tone.

Rick, Chad, and Charlie all looked at Liz with a surprised look and then all of them simultaneously answered, “No”. Liz had a stunned look on her face from their answer. She didn’t realize at that moment that it was the sarcasm of three best friends who knew each other best than anybody including what the tone of their voices really meant.

Rick finally said to Liz “We can say nice things to each other. It’s just not as fun as being mean.”

Charlie looked at all of them and said. “Well, I don’t know about you guys, but all that running earlier made me thirsty. I need a beer, so I’m heading to the club.”

Liz said to Chad and Charlie “I think the both of you owe me one for saving your ass.”

Charlie replied to her. “I guess it’s the least we can do for you, but Chad’s buying. After all, he was the one who got to kiss you.”

"So I guess we're heading back to the club before we call it night" Rick replied.

Liz said to Rick "Yeah, and it will give you a reprieve on being more honest with me, something you should enjoy."

Rick responded "I told you already, you got my one piece of honesty for the night, so giving me a reprieve on being honest isn't going to entice me to go to a club with you."

"How about a chance at getting lucky tonight." Liz said.

Rick smiled and said. "That might do it, but it has to be a definite chance instead of a made-up answer that women like to give a man just to get the man to do what they want them to do."

"I guess you will just have to find out, and you can finish your story some other time."

"At this point I'll probably have to; I won't have a chance to get out of it."

Chad and Charlie start walking away from Rick and Liz going in the direction of wine and song. It had been a long night and the best way to get over it was to be among friends with a good drink.

From a distance Charlie yelled back at Rick and Liz "Will you two hurry up? We're thirsty and I don't have a key anymore."

Rick looked at Liz with a sarcastic smile and said. "That's true, I did have to take it away from him after him and Chad decided to throw a party in the club after hours and half our liquor was missing."

""There's never a dull moment with you guys, is there" She replied back.

"You have no idea, which makes me wonder why you are still hanging around."

"I guess I just like a little excitement in my boring life and there's definitely enough surrounding you."

Rick smiled at her and she smiled back. They just stood there for a moment and looked into each in others eyes finding for the first time since they had met something that seemed to make sense. They had found it with each other that night in the telling of their tragic love stories. Finally they walked away from the park bench and a whole new world seemed to open up for them.

∞∞∞∞∞∞∞∞∞∞∞∞

The next day at the club it was business as usual, the same old crowd, the same stories and the same jokes. The story had already gotten out about what happened with Chad and Charlie the night before so there was lots of harassing for the two of them. Their adventures and less than moral dealings were always a source for comic relief among the patrons of *The Blue's Note* so there was always a story and plenty to talk about.

This night was particular special because it was the return of Gus Thomas on stage and the completion of the blues band he had been playing with for almost forty years. The band members were mainly street and club musicians making a dime here and there, but true to their art and passion. They played for the music; they played the true song of life, the song of their soul. They were not rich men and they were not famous men but they were men of passion and that's what made them true musicians.

Gus had been playing music in this neighborhood for 60 years, ever since he was kid and he could first play the trumpet. As the years went by he started playing one by one with the members of his band and they stayed together. After 30 years they stayed together playing as struggling musicians and perfecting their song. About 15 years before Rick met Gus at *The Blue's Note* when he snuck in to hear the music that was being played there every night. Rick had been curious and one night he had to satisfy it by sneaking in and seeing what went on in The Blue's Note.

Immediately he was transformed and found his *hub in the universe* – he fell in love with the music. Bud wanted to throw him out since he was kid, but Gus talked Bud into letting him stay and began to show Rick what music really was. Gus could play the piano and he knew the mechanics of playing it, but he better trumpet player. He started showing Rick how to play since he was interested in the piano and as soon as Rick touched the ivory keys some deep seeded craftsmanship erupted out of him and he found the other thing in life he was really good at besides basketball.

That was how Rick came to learn the piano and from the first day he started to learn the mechanics of the old Baldwin spinet that sat in the dim lighted corner of the club. A great musical education would soon follow. Rick learned what true music was from Gus and the other band members and as the years went by he became the adopted son of musical genius. Rick and the band became family as he became a surrogate son to them. They played together for next fifteen years playing the sound of their lives. As Rick grew up and gained an education he soon found that the only true learning came from the things that made us passionate.

So everybody was there in usual fashion at the club and as Gus returned from having to deal with the cancer that was eating his body away the band played on. Gus was still sick and knew that his life was coming to an end, but he still found a way to do the one thing that brought out his passion for living, playing his music. Liz had arrived just in time for the Rick and all of Gus' band to start their first set and as the band started to play more and more people started come in as if they were hungry patrons looking for the bread of life. In a way they were because most who came to *The Blue's Note* were looking for something; they were looking for some simple passion to make sense out of their boring lives. They were looking for the music of life and it was in this place that they found it. By the time the band played their first set the club was at full capacity and all anyone could hear was the laughter of the joyful.

The band took a break and Rick greeted Liz with a kiss as he got drinks for all the band members. They laughed and made jokes; they harassed Chad and Charlie a bit

for seemed all was right in the world. *Liz* was starting to feel right at home with all these people that she had just met a few weeks earlier. She even felt comfortable with The Judge whom she had met before and who was there that night enjoying the music of some of best musicians he had ever known.
Everything was good and it seemed that life couldn't get much better.

Liz was beginning to see something of life that she had never known. She was seeing what money could never give you, the simple intoxicating joy of a passionate life filled with laughter and doing something that you truly loved. She began to see the first thing that made Rick a happy person and seeing what the meaning of life for him really was. And just when she thought she knew what it was, the laughter of friends and the music being played, a stranger walked through the door. The stranger would soon introduce her to what it really was that made Rick find his meaning of life.

The stranger was Lee Wayne Johnson. He had one more day in Chicago before he had to leave and he decided to visit the place that helped him find his way in life, *The Blue's Note.* Lee had to be with fellow musicians and there wasn't a musician at the club who didn't know who he was. He also knew who they were because he had played with them with a long time ago. Like Rick he had grown up playing with the same musicians from the old neighborhood, learning his craft, and learning what his true passion was.

Everybody was excited to see him and as Gus and Rick were about to begin their second set they asked Lee to join in so they could jam together again. It had been many years since something like that had happened. Rick and Lee used to jam together when they were younger. Rick played on the sleek and sensual piano and Lee on the devilish and erotic guitar as they used to call the mistress instruments they played with.

As the audience was brought to attention with the famous blues musician about to play with the well known local musician it was evident that all who were in the club that night would be treated to something rare and special. They were about to witness for the last time a combination of perfect and true musicians playing a perfect sound that's not often found. The song was the music of life, a song that is true, passionate, unconfirmed, indiscriminant, and comes straight from the heart.

As Lee strapped on his guitar he looked over at Rick and Gus who he had played with many times before and asked them "So what song should we play?"

They all looked at each other and thought for a moment and like the clarity of heaven shining upon them they all smile for they all knew the song that should be played. Rick spoke up and said "Sweet Home Chicago, it's the perfect song for a moment like this."

Lee started them up with the guitar intro for which he knew very well; he had played the song many times just like they all had. Then he started to sing the first verse and immediately the crowd started to cheer. Sweet Home Chicago was like a theme song to the club and the musicians playing it. It was the song of home and there's other place the gets the kind of love we have for home. For the patrons of this place and the musicians it didn't get better than this.

As they jammed the musicians fell into their element, they were in that place where we all go not often enough. It is the place inside of ourselves where our true being is found - where our true soul is allowed to run free. When we are in this place the rest of the world doesn't matter and we are impervious to her apathetic nature.

Each musician took a solo with the playing their instrument during the song and each fell in sync with one another. The horn section erupted with the fury of heaven and the sweet sound of angelic notes flowed through Lee's guitar and Rick's upright piano. As Rick and Lee both took turns singing a verse Liz couldn't help notice that Rick was filled with pure joy - the childlike innocence of when we discover for the first time the love we have for something.

Liz looked over at Bud who was dancing a little behind the bar and asked "Bud, what is it with playing music on that stage that brings such joy to Rick?"

Bud looked at her with a smile and replied. "Because he's a REAL musician and only through a sweet simple melody can a musician find pure joy. It's just like love, but a different kind than the love you for a mate. When he plays on that stage he is at the very center of his existence where all is right within his world and nothing can be wrong."

"Is it like that for all true musicians." Liz asked Bud?

"Yes it is, buts it's not any different for other artists. All artists have that place and you should already know that.

"What are you talking about?"

"You're a painter, aren't you?"

"Yes I am."

"Then you're an artist and you know that place that I talk about. You may not define it or label it, but you know it.. It's when you find that joy that no one can take away, not even you're father."

"Did Rick already tell you about our conversation?'

"No, but with a little bit of wisdom it's not hard to figure out the obstacles in your way."

"Are you some kind of Psychologist Bud?"

"Far from it, I'm just a man who has watched people day in and day out for forty years After enough watching it's pretty easy to see what gets in the way of people's dreams."

"I guess it's the wisdom of old age that gets us past it, uh?"

"No, it's what we choose to do that's sets us free. For Rick choosing to play the notes found in inspiration upon that stage it was sets him free."

Liz paused for a moment trying to take in all that Bud had said and then as she started to speak Bud cut her off and replied. "You don't have to say anything, just make the right choices." Then he winked at her and

went back to cleaning glasses and dancing to
the song. Liz just smiled and watched as Rick,
Lee, Gus and the rest of the band jammed
forgetting all that was wrong in the world and
remembering a little something of home. They
were finding what made home the best place
to be a place filled with old friends and family,
a place called *The Blue's Note.*

6

The Beauty Within

It's been a little over than a month since Rick and Liz had talked about their past on the park bench and Liz had gotten to see Rick Jam with fellow musicians. They were becoming a lot closer now while becoming the typical couple. They were always together and they had become a big part of each other's lives. It was joyful times for Rick and Liz because they had both found somebody that they could fall in love with. Liz had never know anybody like Rick, somebody so passionate, somebody who was truly happy, and somebody who always found a way to laugh. Rick had a second chance when it came to Liz, a chance to love again and to be loved for all that he was. The last month for them had been good so much so that Liz had taken to staying over at Rick's place most nights even though they had not gotten to that expected level of intimacy that came with spending the night. However things were still good and they trying to figure each other out, but they were happy. Liz still didn't know everything about Rick or he still didn't know that about her. There was still a lot that they gotten around to discussing yet, but Liz would see that night the second thing that made Rick fall into his true line of passion.

As new discoveries would be made between them Liz had become more and more apart of Rick's world, she had become part of his family at the club. That night at the club was a typical night, with the typical conversations and the same playful banter, but this time Liz was doing most of it.

Charlie looked over at Liz and said. "You know Liz, Rick here used to be quite the ladies man back in high school and he went through women like they were going out of style, even when he was in college. If I were you I'd dump his ass and let an actual gentleman take you out."

She smiled and responded back. "And Charlie, who do you suggest that I replace Rick with?"

"I hate to brag, but you would definitely do better with somebody like me" he said.

"Really," Liz replied back. "Well, speaking of finding a gentleman, do you know if there's a service I can call to find one? I think finding one here is still a matter of question."

"Hey, don't be fooled by my rugged good looks".

She smile at him and said "That's nice, but the way I've heard it is Rick had the same girlfriend for most of high school and college, so these rumors that you keep making up aren't going to convince me."

"I'm just trying to point out the fact that." Charlie pointed at Rick, "ugly here might not be the best choice for any future happiness you might be looking for with someone."

"Charlie, are you still jealous that I kissed Chad instead of you that night." Liz asked him

Before his brother Chad could respond Charlie replied. "Yes he is, and rightfully so, because what woman wouldn't want to kiss me?"

Rick spoke up before anybody could and said "Chad that would be a sane woman. Seriously, you need to get your own women, preferably women that you don't have to spend $2.99 a minute to talk to."

Susan came walking over after helping her customer so she could get in the mix of it. Her and Liz had already become good friends while Susan was teaching her, her devilish ways in how to have a good time. It was exciting for Liz because she had never been the strong outgoing type who could influence those around her; she was the shy quiet one that no one ever talked to. Susan would be the one to bring her out of her shell and for Rick it was bring a level of excitement in more ways than one that he had not had in years.

Susan as she walked over to the group at the end of the bar replied "Rick, you need to leave Chad alone. Not everybody can be like you and pick-up any woman in this bar and have a wild night of making love with her."

"I think you have that department covered" he replied with a smile

"I don't hit on every female in this bar and then try to take them home with me she replied then she saw trying to make one of his comments. She replied to him "Chad, don't say anything, and just take that fantasy right out of your head. I'm not a lesbian, I'm bisexual and it's only a state of mind depending on what phase I'm in at that moment."

Rick responded back before Chad could say anything. "Susan, you can say whatever you want, but when you try and get a woman from this club to go home with you after extensive flirting, which for you is every woman you meet here, that makes you a lesbian and it has nothing to do with a state of mind."

"I date men as well; you all know that." She said in a sarcastic tone

"Yes we do, but you also think everything in here is on the menu, and most of the time it tends to be women, so I think that makes you a lesbian"

She gave Rick a dirty look and then responded "No it doesn't, it just makes me bi-sexual which we all know is a fantasy that all you guys around here have about any woman they meet. It's because men hope that there may be a chance for a threesome."

Rick looked at everybody and said. "Okay being one of the only honest guys around I'll tell you this…"

Susan looked at Liz while cutting Rick off and replied "Is there even such a thing as a truly honest guy?"

"I really don't think there is." Liz replied.

Rick paused for a moment and gave Liz a bit of a dirty look then continued with his somewhat profound statement. "I heard that, and no matter what you gals say I'm going to finish my sentence. Yes, as men we're always interested in getting to have a threesome, but when it comes to being bi-sexual you're still gay, so really what's the difference in being bi-sexual or a lesbian?"

Liz looked back at Rick with a Sarcastic smile and replied "Honey, the difference is when you're a lesbian you can't stand to be with a man at all because they can't satisfy you, but if you're bi-sexual then it means that you do like men at least a little bit, and then there's that chance that you'll get to have that little fantasy that all men want."

Everybody else standing around just started laughing and waited for Rick to respond. After a brief pause he replied to her. "Yeah, I still don't know why I put up with you though."

"It's because you love me and just can't stand to live without me."

Rick replied back "Love is just a byproduct and tends to be overrated anyway."

She smiled her devilish smile again and said "But you know you can't live without women, and the sad truth is even though we can't really live without men, we can live without you a little bit longer than you can live without us."

Rick, Chad, and Charlie look at each other while thinking hard for a moment and then responded in unison.

They replied "No, we don't buy that."

Rick then replied "Whatever fantasy you want to tell yourself, but this doesn't mean that women have some magical power over men as you would like to think."

Liz and Susan both responded "Sure there is, it's called sex."

Bud came walking over to the crowd wandering if he was the only helping customers that night. He then replied to the group at the end of the bar. "You know none of you damn kids know even two cent's worth of what love is all about. I've never seen so many amateurs in one room when it comes to love. And before anybody says anything, the reason I know a thing or two about love is not because I'm old, but because I found the secret to keeping the passion going within your relationship ...and keeping a good sex life."

Chad was grossed out by what Bud said at the end of hi little monologue and said to him. "Ah, Bud we don't want to hear anything about sex from you. It's not really your area anymore."

Bud just looked at him with an evil stare. He was trying to say something profound about love, something he had learned over the years from being married for forty of them to one person. Even though Bud was an old curmudgeon he had a lot of insight of what made love work between two people. It took him and his wife a few years to find their balance, but they did and he was better for it even if it was not in a big house with lots of kids. That's what made them survive all these years.

"Chad shut up and listen to me. If you listen for a change and quit running your mouth all the time
then you might actually get a woman. I've been married to the same women for over 40 years and there's still passion in our relationship. We've had to work hard at it, but we both have found a way to stay in love. You see, that's the real answer to lifelong love: finding a way to love that person despite all

their faults or annoyances, and finding a way
be happy with that person. Now if I had to
write a book on love I'd probably title it "Idiots
Galore: The Wrong way to love" I'd have five
case studies for the subject matter with all of
your pictures on the front cover."

Charlie replied to Bud "Damn Bud
that's a harsh thing to say to us. How do you
know we're really all that bad when it comes
to finding love?"

"I listen to your stupid conversations
every night, it's a judgment call. If you want to
know a little truth about love, it's like a fish.
It's boring and annoying trying to catch the
fish. You have to put up one hell of fight that
doesn't even seem worth it when trying to reel
it in, and then it's just stinks, especially when
you have to let it go, or it can just die on you.
I guess in the end love is just like a fish, it
just really stinks, but we wouldn't know what
to do without it."

Bud walked off to help some customers
at the other end of the bar. Susan, Liz, Chad,
and Charlie all just look at each other with
somewhat bewildered looks on their trying to
understand what he was talking about. Each
of them in their own way came to their own
understanding. After a moment or two each of
them smiled at each other showing their

profound understanding of what that old man just said.

Rick spoke up and replied "I don't know about any of you, but I feel better now after that little inspirational speech."

"He really doesn't know me at all." Susan replied.

"Susan, you're never with someone long enough for them to get to know the real you." Rick said.

She responded. "What can I say, I like variety, and by the way the Malone's are here tonight and it's their anniversary"

"Really, how long have they been married"

Fifty years today, and they requested their song from you tonight" She said as she walked to check on her customers

Liz looked over at Rick and asked him "Who are the Malone's, Rick? "

He replied back. "They're this elderly couple who've lived in this neighborhood all their lives and have known everybody around her from the time they were born or since they were children. They have been coming to watch me since I first started playing in this joint."

"Don't forget to tell her that Mrs. Malone is one crazy old broad." Chad replied back.

Rick said. "You only think that because she doesn't like you and she hit you with a broom one time. Frankly, she had every right to; you stole her pie off the window sill as she was trying to cool it."

Chad spoke up in an angry tone and said "she left it there and you know the rule of "finder's keepers." I wasn't just going to leave a perfectly good pie sitting there."

Liz gave Chad a dirty look and said "Chad, you stole an old lady's pie? Honestly what kind of person does that?"

Rick responded before Chad could say anything. He replied "I think stupid is a good description and that Mrs. Malone has every right to keep hating you. After all, the pie was for Mr. Malone's birthday, and considering how hard he's worked all his life at a legitimate job, he really deserved to come home and enjoy the pie his wife made for him."

Chad said back "How was I supposed to know that it was for Mr. Malone's birthday? When I see pie I'm only thinking to myself how good it's going to taste, not if it's for somebody's birthday."

Liz looked shaking her head in the process "That's a sad thing when somebody has to steal a pie from an old lady in order to get something nice from someone or just to feel loved."

"Have you ever had Mrs. Malone's pie? It's worth stealing." Chad replied.

Rick said. "Chad, everybody from the neighborhood at one time or another has had a piece of her pie, but the difference is they don't have to steal it and they still can get a second piece without getting hit by a broom."

Chad just started shaking his head as his way of saying he doesn't care what anybody thought, he was going to do what he wanted to do. Everybody was him was laughing at the story even though it was a story they had all heard a hundred times before. Liz had never it though and it made it even better to tell it again in front of her, also to embarrass Chad.

Liz finally broke up the laughter with an off subject question She asked "Well besides the subject of Chad being a "low-life" who likes to steal Mrs.

Malone's pie, what's the special song they want to hear from you?"

Rick looked at her and replied "I can't tell you that. It will just have to be a surprise to you just like if will be for everybody else in here, but if you like classic big-band and Jazz then you will probably like this song."

"You just have to be difficult don't you" Liz said

"Yeah, because it's fun to be that way" Rick said.

A few minutes later Gus and his band came walking in to get set up for the night. They were back again for another night of playing music for an audience and it just happened to be special for many reasons. The Malone's which had been listening to Gus and Rick play for years was celebrating a lasting love.

They were good people from the neighborhood who never had and prejudices except against those who couldn't put in a hard day's work or find something they love to do or be happy. They were just people that liked good music and a good place with a quiet drink that could make them feel good. *The Blues' Note* was that place and Gus and Rick were their kind of people so it was no surprise that when it came to finding a place to celebrate their fiftieth wedding anniversary they would be found at The Blue's Note where Rick and Gus were playing.

When the band was ready Rick looked out over the crowd and smiled at the Malone's. He started with telling the crowd that there was a special request in honor of a very loving couple who were friends of the neighborhood, it was their fiftieth and he had just the song for them. It was their song, the song that they had courted each other to fifty years ago when they were young lovers with only a world of dreams ahead of them. Mrs. Malone smiled back at Rick and at Gus as well.

The song Rick would play was *As Time Goes By,* made famous by the movie Casablanca. As Rick introduced the couple and finished his introduction he began to play the opening melody if the song. Mr. Malone finally smiled remembering back to when he first took a fancy to his beloved wife and Mrs. Malone started to cry a little bit.

The song was one of those well like songs that nobody couldn't help but like. Everybody in the club started to get into the spirit of the song and couples there that night expressed their affections for one another during Ricks playing of the song. Liz took notice of this as she looked around the room and then looked at the Malone's who were entranced with Rick's inspiring generosity towards them. She looked at Rick and saw it; she saw what made him good at his profession. It wasn't just a talent for playing the squared box of ivories, it was the way he could captivate an audience while inspiring them to be something better even for just a moment.

Liz finally saw the second thing that made her fall for Rick. It was more than just his playing the piano for the people in the audience or those around them. It was his surrender to something artistic, something muse like. He played for hope and inspiration, the great qualities that brought out the best in humanity. Rick surrendered to an art form and it was passion that he played for because it made him feel alive and it rescued him from the melancholy

blues of madmen. He found the true aim of any kind of art form, the inward resurrection of the soul.

Liz watched as he finished playing the song for the Malone's who found the inspiration of love once again by remembering why they had it in the first place and she finally knew. She knew what she had been missing all this time in her art work, what she had never learned, and what Rick had found out years before when he needed it the most. She just smiled at him on stage and knew that this was it; her life was going to change forever.

Later that night after the club was closed Rick and Liz went back to his apartment. As they walked into the apartment they were in the middle of a conversation that kept them both laughing. It was one of their usual conversations that brought out each of their sarcastic sides. Liz was happy and for the first time in years Rick could actually admit that he was feeling like he once did when it seemed that all was right within the world.

As they walked inside his apartment to which Liz was becoming very familiar with now she spoke up. She said "I don't think I've ever known so many people with such comical lives as your friends."

"They do certainly keep everybody laughing. That's probably why I still hang out with them. It certainly isn't for stimulating conversation, although everybody there has their moments" Rick replied back to Liz.

"Yeah, I don't think I've ever heard love compared to a fish before, but I guess that only happens in a bar."

"Hey, anything goes in a bar; especially if its conversation. And that usually means nothing's taboo."

Liz laughed and smiled her small simple smile. She then asked him "Since anything goes when it comes to conversation in a bar, and that should mean honesty, there is something I've been meaning to ask you, and after watching you tonight I really have to know now. How do you do it? How do you inspire so many people through music and make them feel the happiest that they probably have ever been when they're listening to you play?"

Rick looked at her and gave her his small crooked smile when he was amused with her curiosity. He replied. "I wish I could take most of the credit, but it's usually the music speaking through me. You know, Gus told me something a long time ago about music and the inspiration it gives off. You see, music is something that has an emotional connection with us. It doesn't matter what kind of music it is as long as we like it, but it lives in us and lives through us and it connects all living things. That's what inspires us. For a musician, that same inspiration that it gives them projects out to the audience they're playing for, and part of the musician's job is to make sure that happens. I do it because I want the audience to feel the same thing I'm feeling when I play, and when I can make that happen I absolutely love it. That's why I play piano for people in a club and don't want to do anything else. I guess it's the same thing for an artist."

She responded to Rick. "You're right, and art does come in many forms. The thing is, I've never known anybody who does so much in inspiring other people and making them feel good. Perhaps that's why I'm falling in love with you."

Rick kept smiling and said. "That's what an art form is supposed to do, whatever form it comes in. It's supposed to inspire us and it's supposed to make us happy, and that's what we're alive for. It's also supposed to help us find what makes us truly happy, and for me it's the music of life. I also tend to think it's supposed to help us find someone to love. Maybe that's also why I want to be with you."

"You know, with talk like that you might just get lucky tonight."

"Who would've thought that a little bit of truth could actually get you laid instead of some cheap lie? I guess you're just a sucker for the truth, uh?"

Liz paused for a moment and then finally replied with the only thing she could think of "Rick, shut-up and just kiss me."

He leaned in and kissed, he kissed her long and hard with as much passion as he had when he played the piano. As their lips brushed against each other they made their way to the bedroom shedding a piece of clothing from their bodies with each step they took until finally they fell onto his queen size bed. They were still embraced with one another, bodies entangled from their lips to their feet. They remained that way until the sunlight started to creep through the bedroom window the next morning. It was the first time that they made love, giving one of the most cherished parts of themselves to each other.

The next morning they awoke and had their morning coffee together at the breakfast table not saying a word, but letting their eyes say what needed to be said. It was a peaceful morning and they just enjoyed it with each other not wanting to talk the moment away.

Liz got up to start breakfast and as she looked around she asked "You don't have much here in the way of food do you?"

Rick said to her "I don't really keep that much food around here; you know I have to keep up with the whole single man's syndrome of only having beer and ketchup in the fridge. But I do have coffee, which is the most important thing in the food category next to beer.”

Liz looked at him with a sarcastic look and said. “Well, you have to maintain some aspects of a normal guy instead of having the complete *great guy package.*”

“We all have to be something and maintain at least a little bit of what society says is normal.”

“Doesn’t every great artist make themselves great by not fitting into what society says is normal?”

Rick laughed to himself and responded “Sure, but that’s only what we choose to see in them and be inspired by, because we know that we can’t do what they do. We’re inspired by the strength to stand outside the lines, so we don’t see the aspects of normal that they do have. Hell, even Louis Armstrong was a normal guy in that he was a skirt chaser and slept with any woman he could get his hands on.”

She laughed and replied to Rick. “boys will be boys no matter how much of an artist they are.”

“Yeah, we’re kind of built that way. You know, there is something I want to know about you. Are you going to live your dream and be a ‘true blue’ artist?”

Liz looked at Rick and responded. "You still have to make a living at it, and that term "Starving Artist" is very true. Unless you're famous it's kind of hard to make any money selling your work. I don't know if I could really do that. I would like to, though. I would love to go to Europe and be a painter or sculptor. Even doing restoration work I think would be fun. I really hope I could get a scholarship so I could go to Europe, but if I don't I guess I'll have to do something else."

"You're going to let a little thing like money get in the way of doing what you truly love? You're going to let it ruin your chance of being happy? Why give up so easily, especially if it is your passion?"

"I won't give up, but without money I'll have to reevaluate what I should be doing to survive in this life and be happy."

Rick in a sarcastic tone said to her. "You know, Hitler was a painter and because people said he wasn't very good and had no future at it he found something else to do, like trying to take over the world. The sad but funny irony of that is he probably had those people killed later when he was trying to take over the world. But don't you think that the world would've been better off if he hadn't given up so easily trying on to be a painter?

Perhaps he could have been the next Rembrandt instead of a mass murdering shithead."

Liz gave him a dirty look and replied back. "So what are you saying? That if I give up on my dream I'll resort to mass genocide to get revenge for my failure?"

"It's a possibility."

"Kind of an extreme possibility don't you think? "

"It is, but a possibility nonetheless."

"Well I'd like to think that I'm much more of a sane person than that and not the kind of person that resorts to such things.

"Hey, we're all capable of things that we think we can't be capable of. It's just a matter of the right thing pushing us to our breaking point.

"If nobody likes my work and I'm a failure as an artist, then I'll try not to go and kill everybody. But if I do, you'll be the first because I had this stupid conversation with you."

"Fair enough I guess, but just remember that a lot of bad things can happen when you do give up on your dreams, and regret is not something that we should live with. That's probably the main reason I do what I do."

"I do happen to agree with you even though you like to throw out some extreme possibilities of what can happen if we don't live our dreams, but I wouldn't use this kind of argument with my dad."

"Are you saying that your dad doesn't care about living for a passion or fulfilling one's dream?"

Liz sighed and after taking a deep breath she replied to Rick. "It's not that he doesn't believe in those things, he just doesn't see the profit in it. With most things in life there has to be a dollar figure attached to it for him to believe. I can't fault him completely for that kind of mentality, because it did help him to make lots of money and pay for my education."

"Everybody has their own beliefs, and we don't have the right to judge just because they're not our own beliefs, but it's good that you see the bright side to the way your father thinks even though I can tell you don't agree."

"I don't agree with his thinking, but I also want you to know how he thinks if you ever meet him, which by the way you are invited to dinner tomorrow night with my parents and I."

"Why do I have the feeling that you've told them already that I'm coming to dinner tomorrow?"

"I told them that if you didn't have anything to do tomorrow you would probably stop by for dinner and you would like to meet them since we have been seeing each other for the past two months."

Rick laughed to himself and replied to her. "Well it's not a total lie, because it's probably time for me to meet them, especially after last night and yes, I would like to meet them. Do you think they will like me?"

Liz smiled and said to Rick "My mother will, but it may take my dad a little bit of time to warm up to you. Your lifestyles and ways of thinking are very different, and there are certain philosophical conversations that you should avoid with him."

"I'll try to behave myself with your dad, but just remember there are no guarantees in this life, except perhaps death. I don't really think we can escape that."

"Just try and be good. I want them to like you and I want them to be able to see what I see in you."

Rick smiled and kissed her to ease her doubts. He said. "Hey, your parents are only going to see what they want to see in me. All I

can do is be who I am and hope they like me
for that. You're the only one that has to be
satisfied with me, but I'll try and be good so
hopefully your parents will like me."

"That's all I ask."

"One thing's for sure, it's going to be
interesting meeting your parents, which by
the way I hope you at least told them a little
bit about me so there won't be too many
surprises with me."

"I told them a little bit about you, and
yes when you meet them it will be interesting
to say the least."

Rick let out a chuckle and responded to
her "At this point I guess that's all we can say
and leave this to fate, or karma, or chance, I
Ching, or whatever philosophy we choose to
believe that makes us feel good."

"Yeah, I guess that's all we can say on
that."

Rick and Liz stared at each other and
then nodded in agreement. It was a big step for
the both of them. Rick had never gone to meet
someone's parents before; anybody he ever
dated he already knew their parents because
they were from the neighborhood. Liz wanted
her parents to meet the man she was falling in
love with, but mostly she wanted her father, as
naïve and stubborn as he was to see

what she saw in Rick. She wanted him to see
how someone could inspire people to be great
without tearing them down to nothing.

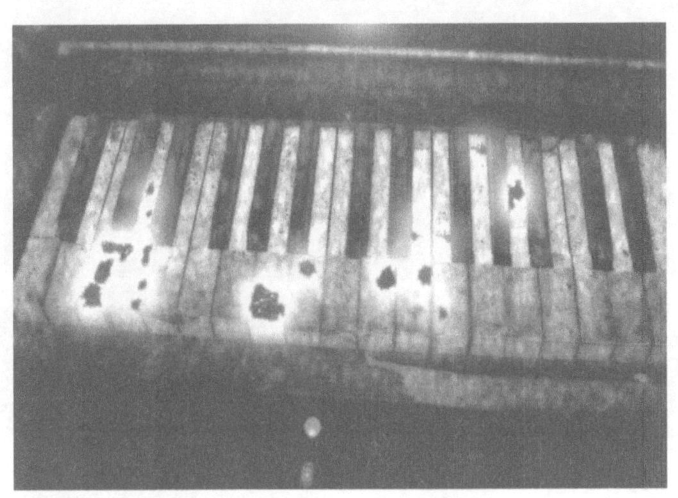

7

It Happens for a Reason

That night Rick was back at the club even though he had the night off so he could have dinner with Liz' parents. He was cleaning up a bit, but mostly he was jamming by himself. He had a song in his head that he could not make sense out of yet. It was just a jazzy melody with no words and only a beginning chord structure. He was an artist trying to make sense out of what he could not see yet, but treading the line between inspiration and insanity. Rick was happy though and in no small way it had to do with Liz so it made easier to dance with inspiration a bit on the piano.

As he was playing Chad and Charlie were having one of their stupid philosophical conversations with the judge while playing dominos and having their daily afternoon whisky sour. After Charlie made a brilliant play Chad got mad and walked over to Rick to find out what he was playing and to harass him like a good friend.

He asked Rick. "So Rick, everything going good in your life these days? You seem awfully happy, even more than usual."

"Yeah, everything is going great just like it has been for the last few years, but thanks for asking."

Charlie walked over and responded before Chad could say anything. He said to Rick. "What my brother in trying to be sly or cool about and is failing to do is ask you if you got some recently because you don't usually hum or whistle unless you're really happy. For you it's usually when you've had sex."

"No, I think you're confusing me with you and Chad. I do whistle when I'm happy….about other things."

Charlie gave him a dirty look and replied. "You're right, we like to hum and whistle a little bit when we've actually had sex with a real girl, but so do you, and after knowing you for about twenty years we know the signs to look for when you've gotten laid. Also it's been awhile for you, and you seem a little more happy than usual, so that means it must have been extra special."

Rick responded in kind by asking. " Is sex all you think about?"

Chad and Charlie both replied at the same time "Well, yeah. We're guys and that's what we do."

"Then why is my sex life so interesting to you?" Rick asked.

Charlie replied back to him Because it's more exciting than our own and it's much better living vicariously through you. You're the piano player, which means you're the sexy one."

Rick thought for a moment and then replied "I know that's true, and I'm glad to know that you can admit it, but you really don't have to keep up with my sex life."

"So are you going to answer the question?"

"And what question is that" Rick replied to Chad.

"You know. Did you get some recently?"

Rick gave him a dirty look and responded "I'm not going tell you, because unlike you, my personal life is not going to be broadcasted in this club. Besides, I'm a gentleman, and we don't tell about what happens in the bedroom."

Charlie started to laugh and then replied "Oh, he must be in love with her because that's never stopped him before."

"Shut up guys." Rick responded to Chard and Charlie. "Just because I don't want to talk about it doesn't mean that I'm in love with her."

The Judge after listening to what he thought was a the stupidest conversation walked over the piano asked Rick "Okay, despite what these two morons," pointing at Chad and Charlie, "are telling you or asking you, how do you really feel about this girl? Is it love?"

"I don't know if its love, but I do know she's great." Rick said. "She makes me feel good; she makes me laugh, and having her in my life just fits."

The Judge replied back to Rick. "Well, I don't know if you know this, but that's called love Rick. For those of us that have known you all these years, you have only talked about one other person that way before."

"I know, and to be honest that's what scares me. I do know that with her it doesn't feel wrong."

The Judge laughed to himself and said to Rick in the Wise old man voice. "Well, love is a strange thing and sometimes the only way you know it is if it doesn't feel wrong. Rick, I think you might actually care for this young woman more than you want to admit to. But I don't blame you for not wanting everybody to know your business, especially in this club. Fiction is always the main theme in any kind of bar garnished with a little exaggeration, and that's not at all unusual in this place...Chad and Charlie."

Charlie looked at him with a sarcastic look and replied. "What can we say? We like stories, and this is a good place for them."

After listening to the whole conversation from behind the bar Bud had to finally ask "What's your favorite kind of story, Charlie-fiction?"

Charlie looked at Bud and said. "It's whatever the hour calls for. Speaking of stories, what's the story behind this song you're playing Rick? I've never heard it before."

Everybody looked at Rick waiting for an answer. He didn't really want to answer because he didn't like how this whole conversation was going. He was getting tired of having his private life broadcasted among the gallery of drunken patrons. Rick: finally responded after a moment's pause and with everybody staring at him.

"If everybody must know, it's a new one that I've been writing. And before any poor assumptions are made, yes I've been inspired by Liz, so that's the story behind this song."

Bud said in a sarcastic tone. "We all know who your inspiration is these days, and it's a good thing that you actually have some because the last thing we need around here is an unhappy piano player depressing the crowd."

"Don't worry about me, Bud. I think you have the market cornered on misery and depression around here. Because of that, anything I do will always seem joyful."

"It's a dirty job, but somebody has to do it" he replied.

Everybody in the bar at the same time started laughing and saying things like things like "that's true" or "you know he's right" to each other. Bud was a cranky old bastard, but he was the clubs cranky old bastard.

The Judge responded. "If you want some advice, don't let your pride get the best of you. Tell her what she means to you."

Old Man Henderson who was sitting in his usually place at the end of the bar shouted to Rick and anybody else that would listen. What you should do is 'mount' her then marry her. Things should always be done in the proper order."

Chad started laughing and said to Rick. "Hey that's good advice; things should be done in a proper order."

"And Chad, that's why you don't have a girl friend. Now Judge, you have good advice, but I'm not going to take advice from the rest of you in this club. I'm not going to take advice from the desperate and lonely which come here day after day to drown their sorrows about long lost love."

"How do you know it's not the woman's fault and we just get screwed over because they can't understand how it should be" Chad asked.

Rick responded to him "This from the man who thought that four women walking in together were lesbians. This is the reason I don't take advice about love from you."

"Now that's really good advice, Rick." said the judge.

"I don't know why you guys are so mean" Chad said.

The Judge replied to him "Because it's more fun that way, and I deserve a chance to be mean to you for all the times you've been in my court and I've let you slide."

Rick said. "Chad, you really are a good guy, but we have to have someone to pick on around here and it just happens to be you."

Charlie trying to keep a serious face said to his little brother "Don't worry little brother. I'll buy you a beer and you can feel better about yourself while drinking away you're sorrows. Many great people in this world like supermodels and rock stars do it every night. Just look at Hugh Hefner. He drinks like fish and is still surrounded by beautiful women."

Rick: looked at everybody and replied "Well, although this conversation has been enlightening, I

have to go. Tonight I'm finally meeting Liz's parents. We're having dinner at their house."

The Judge looked at Rick with a smile and said "That's a big step in your relationship when you have dinner with the parents. That usually means the woman is thinking about the rest of her life with you."

Rick gave him a sarcastic look and said "Let's not get ahead ourselves here and start adding to the rumors that are floating around. Besides, I still like the single life and I'm not interested in being tied down. Remember, the 'mojo' that influences the great philosophy of the piano player is powered by being single. I'd like to still maintain that."

"Someday Rick we all fall hard." The Judge replied. "Remember that's not a bad thing."

Rick: laughed and responded back to "Alright, I'll at least consider that point of view, but if you'll excuse me, I'm off to see if this piano player can be liked in every circle."

Bud replied to his friend. "I don't care what anybody says, you're a hell of a guy, Rick."

Rick looked at him and laughed then gave him one of his famous smiles that said he was a lucky man to have the kind of friends he did. He replied back. "Thanks Bud, at least I'll always be liked by someone," then he walked out the door.

∞∞∞∞∞∞∞∞∞

Later that evening Rick and Liz went to her parent's house for dinner. They lived in a different part of Chicago, further north of downtown where the houses were big and well built. Her parents lived in a neighborhood that showed off money letting everybody know who ventured to that part of the city that the people who lived there were six and seven figure incomes. Liz came from money even though she didn't act like it. Her father was different though, he let everybody know that he had money -that he was rich and powerful.

His vanity had no limits and to his way of thinking he had earned everything he got , it was only right that he could show off and let other people know that he was better. The house that Liz grew up in was classical in its nature and had a very old Victorian feel to it, somewhat out of place for the heart of the Chicago city limits.

As Rick and Liz strolled up to the front door Rick couldn't help but notice the extravagant house. He admired the beauty of the building, but wasn't quite sure that the inside had the same appeal. But he loved Liz so he tried to keep an open mind.

Before they walked inside the house Liz stopped Rick and said "Now remember, there aren't too many things you and my father can talk about without ending up in an argument. Religion and politics are definitely out. If he seems to be antagonistic, just let it go. It's just his way and he's just trying to get you mad."

Rick smiled and said. "You know, your father doesn't sound like a very fun guy. Is there anything we are going to be able to talk about tonight?"

"Probably not, so maybe you shouldn't say too much tonight" she said.

Rick began to laugh as he grabbed her hands to let her know that everything was going to be okay. He looked at her and said "Liz, I'm sure it's going to be fine. They'll like me, and you don't have anything to worry about. Look at me. What's not to like?"

Liz gave him a serious look and said "My dad will find something. Then he'll just harp on it until you get mad so then he can really not like you. That's why I'm telling you it's just best to ignore him and beat him at his own game."

"Well here we are. I guess its game time. No turning back now" Rick replied back to her

"If you did at this point I'd have to hurt you" she said.

Rick and Liz entered the house with the quiet patience of a scared child waiting to get yelled at. Liz wasn't sure what to expect and she was very nervous about the evening, she wanted it to go well and for them to like Rick, but she also knew her father. Rick wasn't the type of guy that he could warm up to; he wasn't a typical business man out to make money. Finally Liz's mother, Mary walked around the corner to meet them at the front door.

"Elizabeth, you did make it and I see you brought your friend. Well, are you going to introduce me to your handsome gentlemen?" Mary said to her.

"Yes, I'll introduce you, but try not be too embarrassing." Liz replied back.

Mary laughed as she hugged her daughter they she replied "Honey, I'm not here to embarrass you. I just want to meet this young man that you've been talking about lately. I'm you mother so that's makes me entitled to meet your friends and embarrass you a little bit if I want."

"Alright mother, this is Rick. He's the one I've been seeing for the last couple of months" Liz said.

Mary looked at Rick and smiled at how handsome he was. She replied "It's very nice to finally meet you. I think you're even more handsome than Elizabeth described."

"Well thank you, it's very nice to meet you Mrs..." Rick said as Mary cut him off before he could finish his sentence

"Oh, please call me Mary. From the way Elizabeth has talked about you, I feel like we already know you in this house

"Okay then, Mary it is" Rick replied back to her.

Mary looked at the both of them and said "Come on in to the living room. Elizabeth's father will be down in a minute." Looking at Rick with a pleasant smile she said "So we've been told that you're a piano player."

Rick responded back and said "Yes, I play piano at *The Blue's Note*. I've been playing there since I was a teenager."

Rick and Liz sat down on the couch in the living room that was filled with artistic pieces and Antiques. Mary took a seat in one of the chairs next to the couch and replied "What kind of music do you play?"

"Mainly jazz and blues with a little bit of classic rock mixed in. I guess I really just play the classics; anything from the 1920's to now that can be played on the piano." Rick answered back.

His answer brought a smile to her face and she replied back to Rick. "That's great, I always wanted to learn the piano, but never did. I was a flute player in college and in the college orchestra."

"Really, it sounds like that was a fun experience."

"Not really, the flute is not a fun instrument. The cool instruments to play on in an orchestra are always the saxophone, and maybe the violin."

Liz replied to Rick before he could say anything "What my mother is not bragging about and has every right to is that she did get to play in the Chicago Symphony for a little while as a replacement. My mother is the only one in this family that has any musical talent, but she has a lot of it to make up for everyone else."

Mary laughed and responded back "I don't think it's worth bragging about, but I guess I was at least good enough to play once or twice for the Chicago Symphony. I will say this, I've always had a reel passion for music even though playing the flute was my mother's idea, but no matter what, it was still a great experience and a lot of fun."

Rick looked at her with a smile happy to find a common ground with her "I think that's the main thing with playing music; really having fun doing it and making sure it's a great experience. That's why I still play and I don't see myself ever giving it up."

About the time Rick was finishing his sentence Edward, Liz's father, came walking into the room. He had a commanding presence and it was something that made everybody in the room get up when he walked in. Rick got out of his seat because Liz did, but he thought it was a bit weird that something like that would happen when somebody came walking in the room. At first he thought it was because Liz and her mother were being polite, but realized that it had to do with the level of respect the Edward silently commanded from people. Rick didn't give it another thought as Edward began to say something.

Edward in a sarcastic tone said. "So what's all this talk I hear about music and the Chicago Symphony? Is someone getting me some free tickets or is that just wishful thinking? I mean, my only daughter could actually get me a present."

Liz replied. "Oh dad, you know I'd get those tickets, but you already have season tickets so it wouldn't do me any good. You'll just have to get something else from me, but only if you're good."

Edward looked at his daughter with a sarcastic look and replied "I'm always good and I really deserve a present."

Liz responded back "I don't know about always being good, but you might actually deserve a present. Although, the jury is still out on that decision!"

Edward laughed and then replied "I've never had a child that gave me so much grief, but I guess that's why I love her so much anyway." He looked at Rick and replies Children are supposed to keep you on your toes and my daughter certainly does. By the way, I'm Edward, Elizabeth's father."

"I'm Rick. It's very nice to meet you." he replied.

Edward responded back "Well, it's very nice to finally meet you. So you're the piano player slash bartender I've been hearing about? So what's life like as a piano player?"

Rick: gave a short smile "It's great. You get to play music every night, and you get to make people feel good and forget about their problems for at least a little while. There's a lot to be said for that, especially if it makes you happy doing it."

Mary looked Edward who had that serious look that let her know that it was down to business. She looked over at Liz and said "Elizabeth, will you help me in the kitchen? I think we should let the men talk before dinner."

"Okay. Besides, I haven't caught up with you lately and would like to do that."

The two women left the room so Edward and Rick could talk. Liz and her mother weren't actually cooking dinner that night, Liz's parents had domestic servants for that, but Mary wanted to get Liz out of the room so Edward could get to know Rick. It was the nature of a concerned father, the part of being a parent where you see if someone is going to be something good for your child. Rick understood that and even though he knew that Edward and he would not necessarily get along with their different views on life, but Rick would do the dance that gave way to parental right.

Both men took a seat and began to talk. Edward asked Rick. "There can't be a lot of money in playing piano in a bar, or is my assumption wrong on that?"

Rick responded "No, there's not a whole lot of money in this business, at least compared to the owner of a fortune 500 company, but there's enough if you don't need a lot of money to live on."

Edward chucked a bit and replied "Hey, I guess the real question is 'what's enough money' or "can there ever be too much of it.'"

Rick smiled and said. "You've got a good point, sir. It's a question that we all have to ask ourselves at some point in life."

Edward got up and walked to the mini bar in the room to pour himself a drink He looked at Rick as he was pour the dink and asked "Rick, would you like a glass of Bourbon before dinner? "

"Sure, a little bourbon is always good" Rick replied back. Edward made two drinks and walked over to hand Rick his. He replied "Elizabeth has told me you're that really good point guard that De Paul had years ago, the one that almost got De Paul into the final round of the tournament two years in row."

Rick said to Edward "I don't know if I was the one that really got the team in the tournament during those seasons. I mean, there were a lot of good players on those teams. However, I did play basketball at De Paul in the early nineties, and I guess I was a pretty good."

"Well, I remember when you made that game winning shot to advance to the final four in '92. My daughter and I were there; it's probably one of the greatest sports moments I've ever had the pleasure of seeing. Why didn't you ever go pro?"

"A serious knee injury the following year in the opening round of the tournament ruined my chances. After two years of reconstructive surgery I decided not to play the game anymore. Also, basketball wasn't something I was interested in anymore."

"That's right. I remember you getting injured and then nothing was ever heard about you again. You were supposed to be one of the top picks in the NBA draft and then you dropped off the face of the earth. What happened to you?"

Rick paused for a moment and went back into his memory to what changed his life. He replied to Edward. "I spent the next two years rehabbing my knee and trying to walk again. Mainly I just disappeared from all that I had ever known before, except playing the piano."

"You must have been doing something all this time, like a career or traveling the world, something adventurous or glamorous?"

"I wish I could tell you yes, but the only thing I did was become a piano player and lose myself in music."

"Did you ever get your degree from De Paul?"

"No, I never did. I left school before my research was complete for my thesis in Psychology."

"So you never graduated or got a degree."

"No I didn't; I left and I never looked back."

"So you quit just like that and never got an education?"

"I did quit college, but I still got an education even though I never received a diploma."

Edward gave a sarcastic laugh and then replied to Rick. "You still need that diploma for your education because without it you're just a dropout. Without it you'll just be a quitter."

Rick smiled at what Edward was trying to do. He was trying to put Rick in his place by letting him know that he was not good enough for his daughter.

Rick played along and answered by asking Edward. "What does a college degree really say about you? Can it show how intelligent you are or if you were actually educated? Maybe all it says is that you completed the requirements to have a degree, but that piece of paper doesn't determine who you are or how intelligent you might be."

"That piece of paper is a requirement for getting a college education; without it you don't have a college education."

"Bill Gates never got a college degree, but he still invented the Windows software and people consider him a pretty smart guy. In fact, he's considered one of the smartest guys in the world."

"Are you trying to convince me that you're intelligent even though you didn't get a college degree? I don't see any major successes to prove that like inventing revolutionary computer software."

Rick paused for a moment to collect his thoughts so he would not say the wrong words. He replied. "No, I'm not trying to convince you of anything. You can come to your own conclusion or opinion about me after tonight. It doesn't matter what I tell you, you'll believe what you want to believe. All I'm saying is that a college degree doesn't mean anything important, or what I personally believe is important in life."

"I guess you can choose any point of view you like, but there is still just one point of view that's the truth" Edward responded back to Rick.

Rick replied to Edward. "Wasn't it John Keats who said 'truth is beauty and beauty is truth?' Although my point of view may not be one you're comfortable with, it's still mine and no matter what I'm going to still just be me."

Edward got a very serious tone in his voice "I guess you're one of those who just likes to disagree with everyone. Or perhaps you're one of those intellectuals that just has to show everybody that you're smarter than they are and that you know best."

Rick responded with a serious tone as well. "I'm not trying to prove that I'm the one person on this earth who knows best for how humanity should think, nor am I trying to be argumentative with you, but I think I'm right in my own personal philosophy and I'm going to stand up for my own beliefs, especially when someone is trying to condemn them."

"I'm not trying to condemn your beliefs or your point of view, but I think you're a little mixed up and could stand to be more objective."

"I didn't realize that I had a problem with being objective, but when it comes to being more objective the same could be said for you."

Edward didn't say respond; he just sat back in his chair to ponder his thoughts. He knew he didn't like Rick and somehow he knew all along. It was the difference in their beliefs and the fact that he couldn't understand how Rick came to believe what he did. The honest truth was that it was fear from something he could not understand. Unless you go through it you can't understand and that was something Rick knew all too well.

Rick knew that Edward didn't like him, but they were both just trying to be gracious for the sake of Liz. For Rick it was just trying to get through an evening without any major problems with someone that he felt could not ever understand what he had been through. Both men just kept their silence for a few moments until one of them broke the silence.

Rick asked Edward. "So what exactly does your company do?"

"We dabble in a lot of things, but mainly we're a technology company. We try to keep up with the latest innovations in technology and capitalize on it."

"Do you like what you do?"

Edward looked at him a very serious look and responded "Do you mean is it fun running my own fortune 500 company? In answer to your question, yes I love it and I couldn't see myself doing anything else. I love big business and being able to find a product that's good for society and capitalize on its use for the world."

Rick responded to Edward. "I think it's good for people to find a profession that makes them happy and also makes them want to go to work every day."

"True, but you still have to be practical about a profession. You have to make enough money to live on. I think the goal for everyone should be to make as much money as possible."

Rick looked at with a serious look and asked him. "So you think having money is going to make someone totally happy? There's more in this life than just money. Why should people be in a job that makes them miserable every day when they come home even if makes them lots of money?"

Edward responded in kind. "Rick, you're going to realize that having money can do a lot more for you than not having it. It will provide more opportunities for you and will give you a greater chance to be happy. Do you honestly think that a street musician is completely happy being poor and barely scraping by?”

Rick paused for a moment and laughed to himself about where the conversation was going. He knew he could stop it right there and avoid any kind of fight, but his pride started to take over. He took a sip of bourbon and replied.

“I’m not saying that every musician doesn’t dream of becoming famous and making millions of dollars so they might not have to worry about anything in life anymore. However, one can still not have worries in life even on limited means. How do you know that every street musician is completely unhappy? There are some out there that are just as content and happy playing on a street corner hardly making any money than in a big concert hall because they do it for the satisfaction of their art.”

“Do you actually know any of these people that are supposedly happy and poor, playing music on the street” Edward asked.

“Yes I do. I’ve known a lot of musicians over the years that fit that description. Most of them are still alive and have been totally happy without making very much money. A lot of them still have other part time gigs besides music, but they’re doing what they have a passion for and for over forty years. The reason I know this is because I grew up with these musicians and it's where I truly learned how to play. You see, they're the true musical geniuses because the passion and inspiration for the music pours out of them onto the audience that listens. When it comes to something like that, money has nothing to do with it."

After a brief pause Edward replied. "Well, inspiration is not going to pay the bills and it certainly doesn't better your situation in life. There are a lot of worries in life that can be taken away with a little bit of money."

Rick: said. "On the last part you're right, if you're talking about your bookie and he's going to break your legs if you don't pay him. Although I tend to think that there are a lot of worries that people have in life that really aren't that big of a deal compared to finding a way to be happy and perhaps keeping our sanity, again money isn't always going to solve those kinds of problems. I know that what I'm talking about is more or less a utopia of sorts, but I think people get confused on what's really important in life, and that creates a lot of the problems that people have."

Edward laughed and replied back. "You know, we all have our delusions of grandeur, but as an intelligent human being we still have to be practical about things. This is one of the things that I have tried to teach my daughter. Its fine to pursue artistic endeavors, but the practical thing is to do a job that will make you enough money to live on in this life."

"So you think there's nothing practical in trying to be the happiest person you can in life"

Edward was starting to get angry and it was beginning to show on his face. He looked at Rick with a stern look and replied "Not at the expense of providing for your family or taking care of loved ones. Your own selfish pursuits cannot outweigh the needs of your family. Sometimes we have to sacrifice the things that might make us happy to ensure something better for loved ones. Making enough money to live on or a lot of money for that fact is just one of those things one does to ensure less worries."

"Well, I think if we keep doing the things that other people need us do at the expense of our own happiness then we drive ourselves to some of the worst things in life like our own emotional destruction or insanity. I'm not saying that we don't sacrifice for other people while sometimes giving up what makes us happy, but we have to be true to ourselves. We have to do what's right for us, and that doesn't make us selfish. All those material things like money or fame or titles aren't things we can take with us. The only thing we have in the end that's worth something is memories with no regret and pride in the life we led."

Edward said to him. "It's a nice thought, but most of the time it's just a delusion made up by those who never had money. That's why artists, writers, and musicians tend to believe in notions like that. When you're starving and out of work those same people use ideas like that as an excuse to keep being lazy and not have to actually work in a practical profession. When you do something like that, all you're doing is taking away from society."

"You don't think that any kind of an artist can actually give something good to society." Rick asked Edward.

Not as much as somebody in commerce, especially when it is the commerce of essential items such as food." Edward replied.

Rick was starting to get a little defensive now. He knew he was being provoked, but what Edward was saying to him was just a ugly thought with Rick. It was as if Edward was attacking who he was as a person, he was attacking his integrity. Rick couldn't help but get mad and lash out so he replied "If it comes down to the choice of living in a world of deluded ideas and notions or selling my soul to the devil spawn of capitalism where I would live each day as a bitter, angry sellout then I'll take the delusion."

Edward looked at directly in the eye and replied "I don't think I like your tone and I would appreciate it if you refrain from calling those who work in capitalistic society as sellouts. We are still exercising our most basic principles of freedom and democracy when it comes to business. If you work hard enough and earn it, then what you earn is yours and doesn't have to be split with anybody else in this country. Don't try and influence me with your Socialist bullshit."

Rick responded. "I wasn't arguing for Socialism, I was merely pointing out that there are better things in life than the endeavors of capitalism. And you're right, the principles of capitalism are just as vital as artistic endeavors under the flag of democracy. All through this conversation you have been antagonizing me to get me to lash out or lose my temper with you. Why?"

Edward gave a small laugh and replied back to Rick. "I'm not going to lie- I am testing you a little bit because I want to see what kind of person you are, and so far I'm not impressed."

"Why, is it because I don't have the same beliefs as you and because I'm a lot different than you are?"

Edward took another sip of bourbon and said. "No, it's because you have no logical sense of what man should do in life. Those little fantasies you have about just doing something that makes you happy at the expense of taking care of the ones you love doesn't have any real logic to it. Those fantasies are just foolish pursuits."

Rick was getting heated in his tone and said. "Who are you to decide what is logical? Just because I believe a little differently than you doesn't mean my thinking is illogical. Besides, the only person I have to take care of in this life is me. I don't have a family and I'm not arguing that when it comes to taking care of your family sometimes we have to sacrifice a little bit of our own happiness. Wait a minute. This isn't about me, is it?"

"What are you talking about?"

"All your ideologies and preaching about what we have to do in life is not really directed towards me is it? This is about what your daughter wants to do with her life and you think I'm some bad influence because I live my life different from how you think a good and wise person should live."

Both Rick and Edward got up from their seats and stood facing each other as they continued to argue. Edward shouted back. "I want my daughter to be realistic about what she needs to do for a career so she can take care of herself."

"So this is about her isn't it"   Edward replied. "No, it's about the both of you, and if you want to live your life in some "being happy all the time fantasy world" without making any money then do so, but I'm not going to have some saloon keeper filling my daughter's head with ideas that's it's okay to pursue entertainment as a way of life and that it's okay to be poor. If I hadn't given up foolish pursuits when I was young and worked hard to build my company, then my family wouldn't have the things that they do and I wouldn't be able to do things that I can."

Rick: asked him. "What part of your soul did you have to sell to get there? Better yet, how much time did you miss spending with your daughter while she was growing up so you could have all this? Sometimes it's not worth it. Sometimes we give up the things that are more important for the things that we foolishly thought were the important things."

Edward yelled at him while pointing his finger and said. ""You have no idea how much I was here for my family all through the years, nor do you have a goddamn clue what I did to get here, so don't throw your judgment at me."

"And you don't have a fucking clue what I've done with my life, so what right do you have to judge me?"

Edward said to Rick "I have the right when it concerns my daughter's happiness. I still have to protect her from those that might take advantage of her or be a bad influence on her. I still have to show her the right choice when it comes to a horrible man that can ruin her life, and so far, you fit the bill."

Rick: replied back. "You can think whatever you want of me, but when it concerns Liz and me, the choice is hers and hers alone. She's an adult, and therefore you don't get to make those decisions anymore for her."

How dare you, you son of a bitch"

"How dare you try to tell me what right I have with my own daughter. If you called yourself a man then you would show me a little bit more respect when it concerns my own daughter. I don't want you to see my daughter anymore, do you understand me?"

Rick responded by shouting at Edward "No, I'm not going to let you dictate that part of my life. The thing is, I'm not trying to disrespect you, but I think you seriously misunderstand what your role is as Liz's father at this point in her life."

About the time Rick finished his sentence Mary and Liz walk into the room to see what all the shouting is about. Both men were still standing and yelling at each other. Mary responded to the anger of both men. "What is all the shouting in here about? Edward, did you start an argument with this young man?"

Liz looked at Rick, with a stern look and asked him. "What are doing arguing with my dad?"

Rick replied. "Edward and I were not arguing, but we were having a little disagreement."

Edward responded with a little sarcasm. "A disagreement! You're practically telling me that I have no place in my daughter's life and I don't love her. I have never had anybody she's dated show me so much disrespect. I want you out of my house right now."

Looked her father with a concerned look and replied "Dad, what are you doing? Just because he disagrees with you doesn't mean you have to throw him out of the house."

Mary responded too. "Edward, she's right. This is uncalled for."

Edward responded in anger. "Shut up Mary. This doesn't concern you. And as for you, daughter of mine, you are forbidden to see this guy anymore. Now get out of my house, Rick."

Mary shut up quickly and looked surprised at Edward's remark. Liz and Rick both had the same look of surprise on their face, they were surprised at the disrespect Edward had for Mary and that he could do such a thing towards her.

Liz replied to her father. "Dad, you can't forbid me to stop seeing him just because you may not like him."

Edward looked at her with the same angry look he had when she would do something wrong as a child. He said to Liz. "I can when I pay for your tuition and rent. I'm not going to have a goddamn bastard like this come into my house and tell me what I need to do with my own daughter and then proceed to insult my way of life."

Liz just stared in disbelief at her father's remark. She loved her father and thought that he might actually love her enough to let her make her own decisions despite money. During the pause as Liz and Mary were staring at Edward Rick walked over to the coat rack started to put on his coat. He shook his head not wanting to believe what had just happened and walked out the door.

Before he got all the way out he said. "I'm just going to say one more thing before I go. That is not what I've been telling you all night and you know it. I'm not trying to disrespect you. All I have been pointing out is that there are different points of view and yours and mine are very different. When it comes to your daughter and me, you don't have any right to tell us how this relationship is going to be or forbid her from seeing me. For God's sake, she's a grown woman. I wanted tonight to go well because I'm falling in love with Liz, but the sad thing is, sir, I think you are bound and determined to hate anybody that might show her a different life than the one you want for her. If you're going to prevent something like that then you don't love her enough."

"Get out of my house right now you son of bitch." Edward replied in anger

Rick looked at Mary and said. "Ma'am thank you for inviting me to dinner." He then looked at Liz giving her a smile and walked at the door.

Edward looked at his daughter and said. "Liz I don't want to hear about him ever again if you still want me to pay for school and your apartment."

Liz replied back. "Shut up, Dad. This isn't your decision and you don't get to forbid me from seeing who I want to see." Edward started to say something, but she stopped him in mid sentence and said. "Don't even think about it Dad. I don't care what you threaten me with at this point. You have no right to interfere with this. I'll walk out right now and you'll never ever see me again. Then I'll tell your partners what you really have planned for the company. You remember, don't you? It's that little tidbit of information that they don't have a clue about."

Liz walked out the door to go after Rick. Edward had a surprised and angry look on his face. He couldn't believe what she said and the fact that she knew that particular secret. At that moment Edward was more scared of what she would do to hurt his company than if she left and never spoke to him again. To say that his priorities were mixed up would be an understatement.

Outside Liz caught up to Rick below the streetlamp as it cast a light shadow across his face. The shadow prevented her from seeing the frustration on his face at her for the way the evening went.

"Rick, where are you going." she asked.

"I'm leaving, because at this point dinner would be a little awkward if I stayed."

"If you were going to leave without me, were you at least going say goodbye to me?"

"No, not really," he responded. "I figured I'd call you tomorrow after everyone had a chance to cool down."

"Look, I'm sorry about my dad, but I told you not to argue with him because that's what he likes to do with people."

"Arguing? Liz, what happened in there was fighting, and the only reason it hadn't come to a fist fight yet was because you and your mother walked in. I'm pretty certain if you hadn't, your father in all of his anger would have tried to hit me because he hated me that much. I think he was determined to hate me before he ever got know me because I don't believe in the same ideals he does."

"Now that's unfair. My dad just doesn't start out hating somebody before he has had a chance to talk with them."

Rick stood there beneath the light with the cool air blowing though his hair and hers. He said. "No, the truth is never unfair, it just stings a bit when we're finally hit with it after spending so much time trying to ignore it. I've been in arguments before. They're just debates over facts and opinions, but your father was literally fighting with me over what I believed. How much did you tell him about me before tonight?"

"I just told him that you were a piano player and a bartender that loved what he did and wasn't trying to make millions of dollars doing it or trying to be famous."

"You see, from just telling him that your father already had a preconceived idea of what kind of person I was because what I am is nothing like him. There is no understanding or objectivity with him"

"It doesn't matter what I told him, and part of what you're saying is true, but you stood toe to toe with him and fought, which is exactly what he wanted you to do. I told you just to let him be that way and ignore it because tonight I wanted them to accept you."

Rick took a moment to collect his thoughts so he wouldn't say anything in complete anger "It doesn't matter if they accept me or not, because your happiness with me is based on your liking me and you accepting me. I did screw up with one thing though. I fought with your father when I should have just swallowed my pride and walked away, but I had to prove that my ideals are just as right despite what people like him may think."

Liz replied to him. "Is that what this is all about, you being right and your own philosophy of life being the right one? If that's it, then you're just as bad as my dad, and I don't want to be with another person like him. I thought you were different. That's why I have been with you all this time."

"I don't have this lifelong mission to make people like your father see that I'm right about how life should be lived. And before you conjure up any notion that I'm like your father then you better stop right there, because I am nothing like him. I'm not saying I'm perfect, and sometimes I get into a pissing contest just for the sake of doing it, even though there's no victory in it."

"I guess with men nothing ever changes. You'll always be those rams that have to butt heads just to prove who is king.

But damn it, Rick, it's not your job to liberate my dad and his screwed up thinking. With somebody like him it's just better to walk away and let him be."

"Or better yet, maybe somebody close to him should stand up and tell him that his attitudes about life and people are wrong. Maybe it's time for you to stand up to him and be who you truly are, despite what he wants you to be. Godamnit, make him see you for who you truly are."

"Look, I can't just can't get into his face like you and make him see who I am and what I want to be in this life. I have to be more subtle about it because I can't change a blind man."

Rick looked with a hard stare and replied to her. "You mean you can't give up his taking care of you or maybe you can't live without someone taking care of you. When we want to be happy... truly happy... then we have to decide what we're willing to sacrifice to truly be happy. We have to decide what's worth more."

"Screw you, you still don't get it."

"Believe me, I do and I do know people like your dad because I see them all the time in the club, and the irony is that they're always looking for some kind of escape. It's

usually found arguing with other patrons over trivial things. You know, your father is right about me in one way. I do live in some sort of fantasy world where having money isn't important and just being the happiest person you can be in
every aspect of your life is what's important. Maybe one day you'll get that and do what it takes for you to achieve that."

She didn't saying, all she could do was look at him with anger and disbelief. She didn't want to believe that he could be right. She knew it though while looking at him with a look of dismay as he turned around and walked away.

Liz: responded "That's it? You're just going to leave now?"

Rick turned around and replied "Yeah, I am because I don't think we need to see each other until things get straight and until I don't feel like hurting you or your father."

He tried to say something else, but just shook his head and started walking until she couldn't see him after he had turned the corner.

B.L.U.E.S.
BLUES

8

What We Never See Coming

The Hospital was cold and depressing as only a hospital could be in reality. As soon as Rick stepped through the front doors he could feel the cold harshness of life's cruel joke upon people, the fact that we all eventually die. It had been over a week since Liz and Rick had last spoken to each other and had their fight. Neither one of them were ready to say something about that night at her parent's place. For Rick it was already becoming the worst week of his life. He was at the hospital visiting Gus, his musical mentor and friend.

Gus had been dying for the last years from prostate cancer. He was in pain most days and
standing up didn't help, but it never stopped him from playing music even when he had to stand up. The pain could be unbearable through the long sets he still continued to do while playing Rick at the club, but music was the one thing that kept him alive and once he gave it up he knew that life for him would be over. This time however the pain caught up with him to the point he couldn't walk and caused him to go into the hospital perhaps for the last time.

Rick found his room that had about four beds in with patients in them and as he stepped inside he thought to himself that death might snatch him since he was losing everything that meant anything to him. He had lost the person he was in love with and now he was losing his mentor and friend. He walked up to Gus who was on an IV drip of pain medication and fighting to keep awake while reading the newspaper. He looked at his friend and said. "If you're just trying to get a break from playing or trying to get attention then you're going to a lot of trouble."

"I wish it was that, but this time I think my prostate is finally going to get the best of me" Gus replied to Rick.

"So is this finally it for you, I know this has been bothering you for a few years and you've been fighting the best you can?"

"I don't know, but it's pretty bad. I can't honestly say if I am going to walk out of this hospital."

Rick took a seat next to the bed and didn't say anything for a moment. He just looked at Gus with a sadden look. He finally replied back "I don't want to hear that you're not going to walk out of here and be playing on that stage again."

"Neither do I." Gus replied. "But the sad simple truth is I don't get to make that choice and you don't either."

"It should be, don't you think"

"It would be nice, but we there is an end to everything and perhaps this is my time."

Rick sat back in his chair and replied in sorrowful tone. "Yeah, but it's too soon."

Gus laughed; he knew how Rick felt for he was one not to take loss very easy. His life had been about loss, from his father walking out when he was a child to his mother dying when he was a teenager, and losing the one time love of his life.   No matter how many times he went through it and the older and more mature he became losing something almost destroyed him. The only thing that could save him was the music he played because it was the music of life - it was his soul being poured out onto the ivory keys.

Gus looked at him and said. "Don't look so glum, loss is just part of the damn game. You take it and let it be the driving force behind your creative soul. Play with the hurt and the sadness and you'll find that the music will set you free, but you know this already because you've been through it."

Rick responded. "Gus I don't need you to be a dad and tell me that everything will be okay. I know the routine, but I still don't want to see you in hear and then one day never you at all. As a friend I get to be a little sad."

"Yes, you do, but I thought you should hear the speech at least once before I go."

Rick smiled at him and responded "There is one thing that I am never short of with my friends...advice. Somebody's always got something to say, but I guess it's better than nobody telling me something."

"Always remember that. The day we don't get that sort of thing is the day we truly feel loss."

Rick smiled again because no matter what Gus was not going to let him leave without feeling better. Gus was not going to let the sadness take over his friend even though he was the one in the hospital dying. That was Gus' way and when he was gone Rick knew that it was that quality that he would miss the most.

Gus looked at Rick with a curious look and asked. "So tell me what happened with your lady friend."

"Why what have you hear" Rick replied to Gus.

"Only that you two were not seeing each other anymore after having a big fight."

"Well I guess news travels fast."

"Bud told me. What happened between you two?"

"We had a fight right after I had a big fight with her dad about my profession and dating his daughter."

"Ah, he told you that you were no good because you didn't care about money in order to be happy."

"Yeah, something like that."

"I guess you weren't good enough for his daughter either because you didn't care about money. I guess he told you to get lost."

"Yeah he did. You seem to know this story already, how is that?"

"Rick, I've been around. I've been playing music for over fifty years and for little money too. You don't think I know what it means to be looked down upon for not having lots of money or caring about not having much."

"What are you trying to say, you've been through something like this before."

"I may have never been married, but I have had my share of heartbreak and I have been let down by people who I though cared about me, but really just cared about status. Money may do that, but it doesn't make you completely happy. But, you already know this."

"Yes I do, but you seem to keep reminding me anyway."

"That's what friends do. Tell me the details of what happened" Gus replied.

Rick sat back in the chair next to the bed told Gus all the sordid details. He told of the conversation he had with Edward and the hurtful things that were said to Liz. He told Gus he knew that he had been provoked, but he couldn't let his pride go and he had to fight with Edward and prove to him that he was right. He told Gus about how he left it Liz and hadn't spoken to her since that night.

Gus looked at him when he was done talking and replied "I thought after all these years and everything you went through the first time you would have learned something."

Rick responded back to Gus. "Look I know that I handled it wrong, but I was right."

"It's not about being right, so what if you were."

"If it's not about being right then what's about."

"What it's about is you being able to show her care about her enough to swallow your pride and play nice so you don't get to be the bad guy."

"What are you talking about?"

Gus looked at him with a stern look and replied. "She knew that her father wasn't going to like you or how you lived your life because it's not what he would do in life. It was about you showing her and her family that you didn't care about what they thought and you didn't have to defend yourself. You could be the better person by not having to fight."

"Why shouldn't I defend myself from somebody telling me that I'm not good?" Rick asked.

Gus replied. "Who cares what they think, why should you have to defend yourself, you who know who you are. If her dad's self esteem is so weak and fragile that he has to tell other people that their no good and he's better then let him live with his own self destruction You be who you are and don't have to explain to anybody what you believe and the reason your life is the way it is."

"Did you ever have to explain to someone why you did what you did with your life?"

"Sure I did, and there were plenty of people that never understood why I choose music for my life and why I didn't care about making lots of money. The thing is I have been happy all my life even when I was on the road almost penniless, but I've always had a song to play and I've always had someone to play music with even a lanky white kid who didn't know much about the piano when I first met him except that he loved the sounds it could make."

"It's a nice memory."

"Yes it is, one of my better ones."

"You know I've never been ashamed of who I am and what I do. Trying to make other people understand that is the hard part."

"Gus laughed and replied back. "It's the unimportant part because it doesn't really matter if other people understand or not, but somehow we convince ourselves that it is."

"I guess that's true."

"Let me ask you this; are you truly happy in life?"

"Yes."

"Are you going to change who you are just because somebody else doesn't get it?"

"No."

"Are you going to stop doing what really makes you happy if someone asks you to even when they don't have the right to?"

"No."

"That's all you have to say. You don't have to explain anything to anybody. Your life is your own and that's all you need to know because you sure as hell can't make someone else see it. People chose to see what they want to see."

Rick smiled and paused for a moment think of all that Gus had said. Gus was right and Rick knew it. Everything he was saying was something Rick already knew, but sometimes we have to hear it out loud and it takes a friend to do that for us.

Rick finally said. "You know, I came here today to make you feel better and instead you become my teacher yet again."

"I feel fine even though I'm here because I already know what's going to happen. You're the one that feels worse because it's a broken heart thing. Broken hearts are always worse than death."

"You're never short of wisdom are you" Rick asked.

"Only for those that need it or have to be reassured by saying it out loud."

"I guess when you teach someone music you teach them about life too" Rick responded.

Gus replied back. "Music is life because for it to be good music it has to be something true of life. Usually when a musician passes on wisdom it's about some aspect of life that is lives played through the notes on that dim lighted stage."

Rick laughed and said. "I guess now you're going to tell me to quit being a jackass and call her."

"No, because you already know that. The choice is yours on how you want to leave it with Liz, but you've been through this before sand if second chances are anything then they the chance for us to make the right choice."

Rick didn't saying anything because he already knew that his stubbornness could destroy anything he might have had that could make him happy. He just needed a friend that had lived his life by making the right choice even if it was hard or never led to great riches. Gus would die a happy man and that was more than most people could say. He would die knowing that the choices he made served him well in the end because there would not be any regrets.

Rick and Gus sat there for awhile sharing memories and talking about old times. The relived the moments of when Rick learned what true music was and how he lived through the music he played. They didn't cry about what was going to eventually happen, but they laughed about the joyful times they had shared. Then they remembered the music they had played and the great friendships that can come out of the most unlikely of moments.

∞∞∞∞∞∞∞∞∞∞∞

Late that evening Rick was back at the club. It was late and not too far from closing time. He and Bud and Susan were cleaning up after Rick finished his sets as the lone musician that night. Chad and Charlie were sitting in their usual places having a conversation with Old Man Henderson. There is not much talking going on except for Chad, Charlie, and Old Man Henderson which reflected the solemn tone of the evening.

Bud was the only one Rick told about the evening at Liz's parents place and he wouldn't even talk about him and Liz in front of anybody that whole week. Gus being in the hospital had hit everybody hard because it was pretty well known that he was not going to leave and his time had finally come. Gus was one of the gang and he was a good friend. He was being missed already so not much was said at the club and no one wanted to say anything as to not make it true. Finally Chad came strolling up to the end of the bar where Rick was.

He said to Rick. "So Rick, we haven't seen Liz around here lately and you haven't said anything about her since you had dinner with her parents. What's going on with you two? Did you screw up with her and get dumped?"

"Why do you automatically assume that I did something wrong and she broke up with me? Maybe she did something and I dumped her, or perhaps I just got tired of her so I broke up with her."

"Because you're a guy, and we're always to blame for whatever problems happen in the relationship. Whether we did anything at all, we're at fault somehow, even if it's just for being a man. So what is it that caused this problem with her? "

Rick: laughed and the replied. "You have a good point, but I really didn't do anything except get into a fight with her father. Now I know this is going to cause some problems, but I don't think I'm totally to blame for anything. She didn't exactly stand up for me even though she knew I had every right to defend myself against her father."

Charlie got in the middle of the conversation and asked Rick. "You don't think she might still be mad at you for fighting with her dad to begin with? "

Rick said. "I'm sure she's mad, but I'm not going to try and find her just to apologize for something I didn't do wrong. Eventually she'll quit being mad, or she'll just stop seeing me. I can only do so much when it comes to mending whatever bridge is between us, and

I'm only going to call her once. If she isn't there or won't return my phone call, then so be it. We just won't be together."

Charlie in his usual sarcastic tone said to Rick. "Yeah that makes sense. Keep being stubborn and wait for the woman to come around because you were the one who was right and she was wrong."

"You don't think I'm doing the right thing?"

"Look, I'm not saying that you didn't have any right to fight with her dad, but if you would have been the bigger person and walked away without escalating the argument, it might not have been so bad and she might not have been so mad at you. Your stubbornness tends to get in the way of you being happy, and be honest, is it really going to fix the problem?"

Rick looked at him with a serious tone and said. "I'll admit my being stubborn sometimes gets in the way of my happiness, and perhaps I should just swallow my pride sometimes. However, I can't just forget what happened. I feel like her father ambushed me, and I did what anybody would do in my place. I defended myself the best way I could. What makes me really mad is the fact that Liz won't stand up to her own father, knowing that he's wrong about her."

Charlie responded. "Maybe she isn't ready to do it yet and you can't do it for her no matter how much you want her to break free. Look, you're the one that everybody looks to when they need help because we all know that you can take care of everybody, but we rely on you because we want your help. Liz may not want that from you yet."

"How come you're the one that has all the answers tonight? I don't think I've ever heard you be this profound before. Usually it's me that has all the answers."

"Even piano players get lost from time to time, and I do have my moments. I'll tell you something else, too. Remember that girl I was seeing a few years ago?"

"Out of the massive number of women you date, no I don't remember her. Actually I don't recall you ever dating anybody in the last few years."

Charlie laughed and responded back. "Yeah, you're funny, but regardless of what you might think in that I'm making her up or she dumped me, it didn't happen that way. I got mad at her for something that at the time seemed like a big deal, but really wasn't and I walked away from her for good. I never tried to call her or go see her hoping that she would come around and see that I was right, but she didn't. For once Chad is actually right about something when it comes to women. They don't just come crawling back. I think they don't do that just to spite men. My pride is what ended her and me, and I wish that I could change that. Buddy I just don't want that to happen to you and see you go through what you did last time when the love of your life walked out."

Rick replied back. "You're right, and I don't want that to happen again either, but I can't stop telling the truth and be somebody else just to please her father and her, too. All the philosophy I know is what I know to be true in life. Part of being me and being true to myself is that I have to be honest with everybody else. If I don't do that then I'm just a hypocrite."

Bud walked over after hearing where the conversation was going and decided give his own advice, something that he thought was better than anything the usual drunks and sarcastic madmen who resided in his place could give. He said to Rick. "Nobody is telling you that you have to be untruthful, but there is a right way and a wrong way to be honest with somebody. I've never known getting into a fight to be the right way, have you?"

Rick: said to Bud "Sometimes the right thing to do is not to back down. We should always fight for the truth."

Bud replied "And did not backing down really solve anything with her dad? As Charlie pointed out, maybe the outcome would have been a lot better if you would've just walked away from her dad's argument. Rick, you may be a pretty smart guy who knows a lot about life, but you still don't know how to walk away from a fight even when you know you should. Your stubbornness does cause problems for you, and there are a lot of happy times you've given away because you didn't want to swallow that pride."

Chad responded in his usual know it all manner by saying "You know he's right, so what are you going to do about Liz? "

Rick: gave everybody a dirty look and responded "What is this, group therapy? Everybody gets to gang up on Rick and solve his problems? "

Charlie laughed and replied. "I guess you can call it that. But hey, we're your friends and that's what we are supposed to do."

Chad before anybody could say anything said "We're only doing what you do for us all the time and that's be our friend, which means you help us solve any problem we might have. It also means that you rely on us just as much as we rely on you. That, my friend, is a two-way street. So are you going to answer my question? "

Liz walked into the door as Chad was finishing his sentence was greeted by Susan. While Rick was thinking about how to respond to Chad's question Liz and Susan started talking. Rick had his back to the door so he didn't see Liz walk in. He argued with his friends for a few moments in response to what they said.

Susan said to Liz. "Hey, we haven't seen you in a while. Is everything okay with you?"

Liz replied. "Yeah I'm doing fine. So I guess everybody around here has all already heard about what happened."

"Honey, everybody's personal life around here is an open book. This is a bar, there's no such thing as privacy."

"Is it okay for me to be here after hours?"

"Sure it is, go on over. I think he'll need to see you."

Liz walked to where the guys were and Rick: still didn't see her because he had his back turned. He was trying to answer another one of Chad's questions. He said to "I don't know Chad. I don't know if we can see each other anymore. I hope that's not the case though, because I love being around her and I haven't felt that way about anybody in a long time. I probably shouldn't have done what I did and I am sorry for it even though I still don't think I was totally in the wrong. I don't have the answer to me and her and maybe there aren't any answers."

While standing almost behind him Liz said before anybody could say anything "I don't know about you, but I would like to try and provide an answer to you and me."

Rick looked at her with a surprised look and said. "So would I. What are you doing here?"

"I wanted to talk you and I also had good news that I wanted you to be the first to hear."

Everybody in the bar looked at Rick and Liz waiting on an answer as if they were part of the question. Liz and Rick looked at everybody who had stopped what they were doing to listen to the conversation between them waiting for them to let them be alone.

Finally Susan spoke up and said. "Alright, everybody out of here. Leave these two alone. They have a lot to talk about."

Rick: looked at Bud and replied "Bud, I'll lock up. Thanks, Susan."

Chad said as everybody was getting up "Why do we have to go, we're just going to hear about it later anyway."

Susan looked at him and said "Chad shut up and get you're but out of here."

The Old Man Henderson "That's okay. Gossip when you're drunk is more entertaining, so I don't need to hear anything right now. Besides, somebody still has a happy hour somewhere."

Susan replied back. "That's good, because you weren't going to get to hear anything anyway, and that includes any gossip later."

Charlie looked at friend as Susan was trying to get everybody out of the bar and said. "Rick, just be honest with her and yourself. Don't let that stubbornness get in the way."

The group walked towards the door and was making comments to one another about having to leave as Liz took a seat at the bar. Susan was having a hard time getting Old Man Henderson and Chad out the door. It brought a smile to both Rick and Liz's face as she tried to wrangle two big kids from getting in the way.

As they getting out of the bar Chad said to the group "I feel like pancakes. We should go get some breakfast before the 'drunk crowd' shows up at the diner."

"Is eating all you think about besides getting laid?" Charlie asked his brother

Chad replied. "What other fun things are there? There are only so many fun things to do in life and food and sex are probably at the top of the list."

Charlie looked at his brother with a sarcastic look and asked. "How is it that I'm related to you? I always wonder why God cursed me with being related to you?"

"Just for that you can buy everybody breakfast tonight".

Susan said to Chad. "In that case I'm definitely joining you for breakfast."

Bud had to put his thoughts in and replied "I think breakfast on you is a good reward for having to listen to your stupid conversations every night. I guess I'll be joining you guys."

Then Old Man Henderson said. "Hey, if you guys are buying breakfast then happy hour can wait, but can we stop buy the liquor store first? I need a little Irish coffee with my eggs."

Charlie said to the group "Hey, I'm not buying breakfast for everybody. Since when we do actually listen to my little brother?"

His brother replied to him "Come on Charlie. You have the money because you sold all your Phantom of the Opera tickets tonight and we're going to the diner where Dallas that cute waitress you like to flirt with works."

Charlie gave his brother a dirty look and said "You're such an idiot. I don't know why Mom didn't leave you at the zoo that time. You would have fit right in with the monkeys."

The group finally got out the door so Rick and Liz were the only ones left in the bar. They were both laughing at the comic routine Rick's friend went through just to leave and get something to eat. Rick: look at Liz with a smile his face and said "I don't know why I still hang around these people anymore. Sometimes I feel like just taking off and never returning, but then I might miss them."

She replied to him. "You would miss them because they're family and believe or not they do take care of you. From what I heard, they know exactly what to say to you when you need to hear it. When it comes to people you love that's what they're supposed to do for you."

"I guess you're right. So what brings you into my door this time?"

Liz took the cup of coffee from Rick that he handed her and said to him "I wanted to see you and tell you what I think is some good news. I also thought we both have had enough time to cool off. By the way, I did get your message."

He said to her as he poured himself a cup of coffee "We probably both have a few things to say to each to other. Before we go on, I should apologize for my behavior with your father. I still don't necessarily think I was wrong in what I said, but the way I handled everything was wrong and I think you should know that."

"You were right in what you said and you were right about me."

"I wasn't trying to insult you, I was just angry because you didn't defend me."

"I know you weren't. You're right, I've never been any better than a servant when it came to my dad. Making him understand what I want for my life has been a long time coming. That's why I had a very long talk with him this week about my future and what my plans are."

"How did he take it?"

Liz gave out a small laugh and said to Rick. "Well, he wasn't pleased, and I don't think he's going to waste his money on me anymore as he put it. However, I did make him understand that what he wants for me and what I want are two different things. The funny thing is he already had an office for me at his company, and apparently I was supposed to start in the next couple of weeks. Anyway, you were certainly the catalyst for that discussion with my dad and for me resigning before I even started."

"I've been that for certain things over the years and although I'm sorry about how it happened, I'm glad that it did. It sounds like to me it might end up being a good thing."

"I think it's going to be a good thing, and I also should have defended you or at least pulled you back before you really got carried away."

Rick began to laugh a little bit. It was the first time in a while that he could do that with her, he thought to himself. He could finally laugh at his stupidity with her. Then he replied to her "Yeah, I definitely got carried away. You got to see me when I howl at the moon a little bit. Those are not exactly my finer moments, but then again I think we all have moments like that."

She smiled at Rick and said. "You're right about that, and it felt pretty good having one of those moments with my dad, as I'm sure it felt good for you when you had that moment with him."

"Your dad, my new best friend; Oh yeah it felt pretty good. I can't lie about that" Rick said sarcastically to her.

Liz looked at him with a seriousness and sincerity that she had not had before with him. She said "Rick, I have lived for the most part a sheltered life and did what my parents wanted me to do. De Paul was more or less a compromise as long as I got a business degree. I was supposed to go to University of Chicago because my dad and mom went there. College was supposed to be my breaking free period and I have done that to an extent, but there are still some things that my dad has still had some say about in my life. The point is, it's not as easy for me to stand up and rebel. With my dad and the life he has provided for his family, it's very hard to go against what he wants for us. You don't have any ties, so you have nothing to lose by standing up to him."

Rick replied to her as she took a sip of coffee. "You have a point, although the difference between you and me is that I've been standing on my own two feet without any help for a long time and you haven't. Don't get me wrong I'm not criticizing you for how it's been in your life, and believe me, I can understand why your life has been the way it has been, but there does come a time when we have to rise up and break free so we can find who we truly are."

She smiled and replied to him "And that's what I'm doing now because it's time. This whole thing sounds like something out of a movie. You know it's the kind where some small town girl goes off to the big city to find her dream when her parents don't approve. Then she meets somebody who shows her what life is all about, and in the end she has to make that choice to live life under the submission of her family or break free to live her dream and her own life."

"Isn't it funny how stories in movies truly mirror how life really is sometimes?

Enough of that, I want to know what this good news of yours is.”

Liz continued with what she was saying “I’ll get to that in a minute because there’s something else I want you to know. Now I don’t want you to think that I’m some silly school girl who’s easily infatuated with the first charming and funny guy that comes along. I may be easily inspired, but I’m still critical and objective when it comes to men. The thing is Rick, the past two months have been probably the best time in my life, at least that I can remember. I’m in love with you and I think I have been since the first time I ever heard you play. The night you played for the Malone’s and I saw how you can touch people inside with music just confirmed for me how much I’m in love with you. I’ve never known anybody like you or known anybody that inspires me the way you do or makes me feel beautiful inside or who can make me feel like I can do anything.”

Rick looked at her with sincerity and replied. “I think I’ve known for awhile, and to tell the truth I haven’t done all those things to try and make you fall in love with me. I did it because I believe in you and I want you to be happy. I want you to find what I found and the reason I want all this for you is because I have fallen for you. These days I really can't see myself living without you. Perhaps that's why I've been so nutty lately."

She said to him "Well then, here's my good news. I got the scholarship to the art school in Paris. I'm getting my chance to live my dream and to do something for me."

Rick got excited and his smile came back. He said to her "That's great! I had no doubt that you would get this chance. I bet the excitement is just overflowing inside of you right now."

Liz said to Rick with excitement "Believe me, ever since I got the letter I've just wanted to scream for joy and tell everybody I saw, but I've actually waited because I wanted you to be the first one to hear about it."

"So far I'm the only one who knows?"

She smiled and replied "Yeah, not even my parents know, which will be interesting when I tell them because my dad thought I wouldn't get the scholarship and then I'd be forced to work for him. I wanted to tell you first because you're the one who's believed in me the most, and I want you to come with me. I don't want to do it alone. I want to do it with somebody that I love."

"I can't go with you, Liz. This is something you have to do on your own"

Liz paused for a moment and just looked kind of shocked at Rick. Then she said. "That was so not the response I was expecting. I want you to be with me as I take this step. I'm not asking you to live my life for me, but just stand by me. After being with you I can't see being without you. Doesn't that count for something?"

Rick looked at her with the best sincere look that he could give her and said. "It counts for a lot and it makes me feel good to hear you say all this, but I can't go with you. No matter how much I can't live without you or how much I miss being around you, or hearing your laugh everyday and seeing your smile light up the room I can't go with you."

"Why not, if you can't live without me then why won't you go with me?"

"Because this is my home and this is where I belong."

Liz smiled trying to hide a few tears and said "Didn't you tell me once that for some people home is where they hang their hat- that for them home is never one place? Does is really matter where you are as long as we can be together?"

"You're right to an extent, but let me finish. Part of the philosophy I've acquired over the years is knowing that some people are meant to wander and find different places to make a difference. On the other hand, some are meant to stay in one place and that's where they find happiness and make a difference. I found out a long time ago that was me, and I would never leave this place. I wouldn't even want to because I am truly happy when I'm here. It's my *hub in the universe!*"

"How can you say that when you've never seen the rest of the world or experienced everything you can from it." Liz asked him?

Rick walked out from behind the bar and sat down on the bar stool next to her then he replied "I'm not saying that we don't visit other places, but there is one place that we truly call home and always return to. The only way you can know that is if you do go and see what's outside your home. I've done that. I've been to places that I thought I would never go to, and even though I haven't seen all that I would like to, I do know where my home is. You haven't. You haven't been outside of this place to know if you will one day call this your true home."

"Have you ever been to Paris" Liz asked him.

"No, I haven't yet, but maybe someday I will get there. And there's another reason why I can't go with you. You getting to go to Paris and have a chance at being a professional artist is your day in the sun, and I can't interfere with that. I had mine with basketball and although I'm a little disappointed that I never got to play pro basketball, but I don't have any regrets about the chance I got and what happened to me. This is your chance to find out how bright you can shine in the spotlight and I can't be with you for that. Sure, it might be nice if we were together while you do this, but the journey of finding ourselves and what makes us happy has to be done alone."

"Wasn't Linda with you and standing by your side while you were playing basketball?"

Rick said "Yeah, she was, but playing basketball at De Paul wasn't where I found myself. That other thing I was going to be honest about on the park bench was this; it was after I was done playing and after Linda had left that I found myself, but the journey that I took in doing that was done alone. Through all the depression and through all the agony that I endured in that part of my life, I still had to do it all alone. Sure, there were my friends that were nearby and would get me a cup of coffee with some aspirin if I was hung-over, but in the end I was the only one that could find the answer to who I really was and what made me completely happy."

"You're right about people having to figure out who they are and what they want on their own, but I still want you nearby to make me feel happy and safe, to tell me that everything is going to be okay and just because I want to be with you. I want to know something. What do you really have here that you couldn't walk away from, especially for love?"

Rick: gave a bit of a sarcastic laugh and said. "Now that's kind of a tricky answer because when it comes to love there really isn't anything that we shouldn't be able to do for it, and yes I'm one those that could walk away from a life where I'm happy if a loved one asked me to, but there's a flip side to this issue that were talking about. First of all, I could give you a thousand inspirational speeches about finding yourself and what makes you happy, but they're all going to have the same point: you're the only one who can do it and you usually have to do it alone. Now the hard thing about loving someone is setting them free or letting them go. That's the true test of loving someone! If you want to know how much I'm in love with you, I love you enough to do that."

Liz gave a Rick a sad look and said. "I don't understand. Are you trying to tell me that for us to be together we have to give in to that old cliché where if you love somebody set them free and if they come back it was mean to be?"

Rick paused for a moment and replied "Something like that, but I also don't want to be responsible for you having to give up something that could be your dream come true, or your destiny if you will. I understand that loved ones sacrifice for each other all the time, but they can't sacrifice their own happiness or the things that make them complete because if we do something like that then we're destroying who we are and I don't think somebody who claims to love you can ask you to do that."

"Now be honest with me are you just telling me all this because you don't want to live in Paris with me because if that's the truth then just tell me. I want you to be honest with me."

Rick: replied back in a defensive tone. "Okay, you're right, I don't really want to live in Paris, but that's not a reflection on you or me or not wanting to be with you. However, I'm not asking you to stay here for me, because if I love you like I've said before, then I can't. My little philosophical speech is not something I'm making up just to let you down easy. I mean every word I'm telling you, and as much as I love you and want you to stay, I have to let you go so you can find what makes you happy…what makes you complete. The only way to find those things is to go out there, take a journey into the world, and to take that journey into ourselves."

"You know when you want something bad it's never easy and I guess I'm still one of those people who are still naive enough to believe that when two people love each other it's going to be easy, because love is all you need."

Rick: laughed and said to her. "That's the thing *The Beatles* never explained in their song. Besides, when is it ever easy when it comes to the things we want or the things that might be good for us? It kind of reminds me of that old Buddhist philosophy, the harder the journey the greater the reward. But I'll tell you the real bitch of being in love. It's when you get a second chance and you still have to let them go. For me, I haven't felt this way in a long time and I never thought I would. I thought for longest time after Linda that there would never be anybody who could make me fall in love, but you did. And I don't want to let you go, but I know I have to."

Liz paused for a moment to collect her thoughts then said "I know you're right and that this journey is mine and mine alone, but I want to know something from you. With everything you know and have learned over the years; with all your philosophies of life, does it ever take you out of here, out of Chicago? Do you ever broaden your horizons a little bit anymore, or do you use all this philosophy as an excuse just to hide the fact that you're hiding from having to try something new?"

Rick replied to her in an angered tone, "Hiding! You think I'm hiding in this place?"

"If we're being honest with each other then yes, I do. Think about it. Ever since Linda, have you ever gone anywhere outside Chicago? Have you ever left here to see the world?"

"Liz. I've been to a lot of places in this world. Let's remember this isn't about me. This is about you and the journey you need to take."

"You might have visited a lot of places, but that was before she left you. Be honest.

You haven't gone anywhere but here since then. If this is about the both of us finding ourselves and being complete so that one day we might be together, then be totally honest with yourself"

"It's not hiding. I just don't have any reason to go anywhere else."

"That's just a made up excuse to convince yourself that you're not really hiding from the rest of the world. If your gonna talk about second chances, then second chances mean you have to get up after you've been knocked down and try again."

"Goddamnit, I am not hiding! Quit making this about me!"

"Liz If you're getting that mad over what I'm saying, then maybe I'm right, and this isn't only about me. This is about both of us and whether we have a future together."

They both just paused and didn't say anything to each other for a few moments. Rick got off the his bar stool as did Liz so they wouldn't be so close to each other when they were angry. Finally Liz asked Rick "Are you not going to say anything now? If you're just going to stand there and be mad then this is never going to work. Like you said, the truth stings sometimes."

Rick looked at her as serious as could be and replied "Okay, maybe you're right. Let's say I've been using my life here as an excuse not to try again, but I'm still right about what I've said to you. It's funny, we can be so right about other people, and I've learned to have good judgment about people after being here so many years, but maybe I can't see myself as clearly as I always thought."

Liz replied "Rick, I'm not trying to know everything about you and put you in your place, but I want us to be to be totally honest with each other. You're right about me, and you were right about my dad. As much as I want you to go with me to Paris, you're right to say I have to do this alone, but if I'm going take a chance and evolve into something better than myself, then you have practice what you preach."

Rick: smiled and replied to Liz. "I guess I can't get off the hook with this one, especially with all the preaching I've done up to this point."

"No you can't, because if we're going to be together someday, then we have to both be at that point where we're ready for it, and I for one am looking forward to that day."

"I guess when two people love each other then they keep each other in check, don't they?"

"You got it, piano man."

"Then I'll make this promise to you. Although this is my Hub in the Universe, my universe could get a little bit bigger and maybe one day it will be our time. You know I can't go with you though, right?"

"I know, and all I want from you is not to hide away from the world, but I don't want you to change from the person I fell for. You're picking yourself up again after being kicked down by taking a chance on me. I could be really, really psycho and boil your pet alive just to get you to love me."

"Well I'll be sure to keep the family pet away from you if you ever get really mad at me. Even though I can't go with you, you're going to do just fine."

"I hope so, but I'm still going to need you to believe in me if I'm going to succeed at this."

Rick hugged her and held her tight. He said to her "I'll always believe in you, and that will never change, but you don't need me and you never have. Liz, I don't want to let you go, but I know I have to. You've made that kind of difference in my life. You should know that after you leave here tonight there won't be a day that I won't look to that door waiting for you to walk back through it into my life again."

"Someday when its time, but I won't say goodbye, just I'll see you later. You are going to see me off at the airport aren't you?"

They let go of their embrace and Rick said to her "I'll pick you up and I'll see you off, you can count on that. I won't say goodbye to you either, only I'll see you later. Hey, I might even say I love you."

"That's what I need to hear from you."

"Yeah, you're not any different from any other women I've ever known. All you need to hear is, *I love you.*" Rick said to Liz in a sarcastic tone.

"You still don't know me completely yet, but maybe someday you will."

"You know, there is one thing that we haven't done yet that I would like to do and that's dance with you. It just so happens that I have a jukebox in here so how about it?"

"You got it, so why don't you play it for me Sam?"

Rick hit the Jukebox trying to be funny as he did his best "Fonzi" impression. The jukebox actually started playing a song. Now

Rick didn't pick the song because the buttons that selected the songs didn't really work; all you could do was hit start and a song would start playing. The song that started playing was *If you don't know me by know* by Harold Melvin and the Blue Notes.

Rick smiled and replied to Liz Ah, the ironies of love, I guess we can't ever escape them."

She smiled and replied back. "Certainly not in this place"

They stood there dancing to the song and holding each other tight, trying not to let go of each other. They both knew they had to eventually, If love is to ever survive its always seen in what we're willing to let go so that one day it might return. The truth is in a stupid cliché, but more of a truth than most things. Rick and Liz didn't think of their words to each other, they weren't thinking of tomorrow; they held on to that time and place where in those few minutes while the song played they belonged to each other and were free from all abstractions.

9

An Ending to the Beginning

Sitting in the Chicago O'Hare Airport with Liz Rick thought to himself, we as people move within shadows and a trudging pace. It's not unusual for people to keep moving without noticing the little things that make us happy. Sitting next to Liz he took notice of something that made him happy, but was not his too keep. He had taken Liz to the airport as she waited to board a plane bound for Paris France. Rick didn't really want her to go, but he knew that he couldn't go with her to Paris. He was as certain as breathing without thought. For them to be happy with each other it would have to be in the right time and that time is never in an instant.

The flight was an early one and they had not gotten much sleep the night before with all they had to talk about while finding a way to still love each other. It was something that they had to hold onto in order to make sense out of everything that they had been through with each other. What they were holding onto would be the only thing that kept them alive as one instead of two separate longing souls, it was their hope.

They just sat there in a couple of empty chairs by the departing gate waiting for her to board while watching the other planes take off and people hurry through the terminals. They didn't say anything to each other while holding hands trying to comfort each other in that already awkward moment of leaving. Rick and Liz didn't want to say anything that might ruin the last few moments they had with each other. Liz finally looked over at Rick giving him a bit of a sarcastic smile then she said "You can still come with me, it's not too late."

Rick replied. "You can still stay here, it's not too late. But we both know that you have to go and I have to stay or we will know for sure if we will be right for each other in the time to come."

"Trying to find complete happiness is never easy, I don't like having to find the patience to find out." Liz said.

Rick squeezed her hand and looked deep into her eyes that were swimming in a sea of emotion. Then he said. "I don't like having to have that patience either, it's the hardest part of holding onto love and getting second chances."

She didn't say anything to Rick, but she continued to look inside of him at what he held close to his heart; it was the burden of loving and letting go, the burden of second chances. They attendants finally called for passengers to start boarding. She didn't want to get on immediately waiting to see if her parents would actually show up and see her off. After a few minutes of waiting and letting other people board the plane her parents finally arrived to say goodbye to her.

Rick didn't want to be in the way so he hugged her and kissed her saying his so-called goodbye, "see you later," before her parents walked over. She had one request from him other than writing to her. She asked him that before he started playing his first set at the club he would look up at the door to see if she would walk in. He smiled and said yes then turned and walked away.

Rick walked past her parents and acknowledged them, but didn't say anything. Edward just gave him a dirty look and looked down upon him, but Mary on the other hand walked over and hugged him kissing him on the cheek to let him know that everything was okay. She wanted to let him know that everything would be okay and she would love him because her daughter did, that was good enough for her.

Rick didn't leave right away. He watched as she said goodbye to her parents and then watched as she boarded her plane. Liz turned around before she entered the jet- way and as she saw him standing off in the distance she blew him a kiss while letting him see her smile once again. Rick smiled at her and just held his hand over his heart to let
her know once again how he felt about her. He stayed long enough to see her plane back away and leave. Then he turned around and walked out of the airport hoping to never have to say goodbye again to someone that he loved in the place where planes flew out to different parts of the world. The carried people's loved ones and of them carried his to Paris France.

Rick disappeared for a couple of days after seeing Liz off at the airport. He was in a solemn mood and he had to collect his thoughts about everything that had happened over the past two weeks. It was like a dream because it happened so fast - one day he and Liz were happy without a care in the world and it seemed like the next day she was gone. They loved, they fought, and they had let go for the hope that one day they would love again.

After a couple of days Rick went back to *The Blue's Note* and it was business as usual. He went back to his friends, his family, and being the piano player that everybody just talks about, but somehow never really knows. Liz was not one of those people. Over the course of two months she had gotten inside and she saw who he really was. Liz had taken with her the strength and courage to live her life that only someone who had been to the bottom of the abyss and found the salvation to keep living could give to someone. It was this that Rick would always take with him and remember most about her.

Rick stood behind the bar with a stack of papers ignoring everyone as he concentrated on his new venture in life. Nobody had really said anything to him trying to keep their distance as to let him grieve if he needed to. Finally Charlie and Chad walked over and sat on the bar stools in front of him.

Charlie asked Rick. "So is Liz gone now?"

"Yeah, I dropped her off at the airport this morning so she won't be around anymore."

"Are you sad? I know I'd be sad if my girlfriend left me." Chad said Rick.

Before Rick could answer Charlie replied to his brother. "You're sad when any woman wants to get away from you, even if she's as big as the Titanic and got severely beat by the ugly tree. And just for clarification, she didn't leave him; she just went to Europe for art school. Can't you show a little sympathy?"

Rick: laughed at his friends and said. "It's alright guys. Yes, I'm a little sad because I told her what I needed to say to her and I still had to let her go, but that's the game of love sometimes."

"What are you going to do now?" Charlie asked Rick.

Rick responded. "Well, I am going to have a stiff drink tonight, and I'm actually going to start writing again and I am going to keep living. I'm also going to thank God for second chances and just for an added bonus I'm going to confession tomorrow. I'm sure I'll have to say a few extra Hail Mary's for having friends like you."

Chad asked Rick. "What are all the papers for?"

"If you must know, they're what I need to get back into De Paul so I can finish my degree. It's time to stop hiding and broaden my horizons a little bit. Boys, there's a bigger world out there and I'd like to see it."

Charlie replied. "You're not on some weird spiritual kick are you? If you start chanting and becoming a vegetarian then I'm not going to hang out with you anymore."

Rick said Charlie "So that's what it'll take to make you leave? Well, I should have done this years ago. I'm just kidding, Charlie. This is about becoming a better person and not hiding here anymore. I can still be the happiest I can be when I'm here, but I can't hide here anymore. I'm going to make some changes for the better in my life."

Charlie said. "That's a good plan, Rick. Chad and I are making some changes as well. We're getting out of the 'back of a van flea market business' and we're going to open up a legitimate ticket shop. Besides, the Judge is retiring, so we won't have our inside connection in the courts anymore. Yeah, it's time to get a legitimate job now."

Rick laughed at his friend's remark and said. "I think that's been a long 'time coming Charlie, but I'm glad to hear that you two have decided that it's time. Wouldn't do you much good to end up in jail again since you really don't have a 'bail fund' anymore?"

Charlie said to Rick. "Like you, it's time for us to make some big changes in our lives. But the fact that we really can't afford to go to jail anymore has had a lot of influence on us."

Susan and Bud made their way over to the conversation at the corner of the bar. They too were interested with what was happening with Rick now that Liz was gone. Susan put her hands on Rick's shoulders to lend a comforting hand him and then leans in to tell him something Susan asked him "Are you going to be alright now that she's gone?"

Rick: replied to her. "Yeah, I'm going to be okay, and I'm going to go on being me. She made a difference, but she made a better person out of me and I'm going to let that show in my music and my life."

Susan said in a comforting tone which was unusual for her "I know we're all going to miss her around here, but don't let the man she brought out in you go away. I for one have enjoyed him being around."

Susan hugged Rick and as they hugged Rick said. "I won't Susan, and that also means you can't let the person you've become go away either."

Susan replied back. "Just to let you know, I've been inspired by both of you so I am going to make some changes in my life, but only for the better. For one, I'm only going to be with one person at a time in a relationship, but no matter what, I don't think I could ever stop being me. I have to in this place so I can keep some balance between sane people and morons."

"You should know by now that there's no such thing as sane people in this place" Rick replied.

Bud who had been standing there with a scowl on his face finally put his two cents in. He said "That was never truer until all of you started coming here, and since everybody is making changes in their life I better not see my sales go down or I'm just going to have to make you change back so this place can be like it always has been."

Rick said. "Don't worry Bud, we won't let the worst thing in the world for you happen. And remember, you're not that lucky to get rid of all of us while seeing your place change for the worst."

Bud looked at his best friend who was like a son to him with a half cocked smile and said. "I know that's true, and believe it or not, I probably wouldn't have it any other way. Now I'm not going to admit that ever again so if you'll excuse me I have customers to tend to." Bud then walked away, but only a few feet away to help some customers for he would never be far off from the people that he cared about the most.

Rick looked at his friends, the people that were his family and said to them "You know, it's a long and strange journey we take in life, but I think that's the best part of it."

"It's The Music of Life" Chad said.

"What did you say" Rick asked in a surprised tone?

Chad looked at Rick and then to everyone else who had surprised looked upon their faces and replied "The journey in life, it's the Music of Life. Life, like a song, has its many verses to the same story. Sometimes we have different themes to the same story and we go through our ups and downs just like the notes reflect by going up and down. We have our climatic times that help us see the true meaning of the story, but in the end we come to a realization that we've never had before. The story is life and in it is the Music of Life."

Everybody just looked at him not wanting to believe that Chad was capable of saying such a profound thing. Rick smiled a little at what his friend said because there was truth in it. Susan let out a small laugh at what Chad said and then started shaking her finger at him with excitement because Chad finally said something intelligent and poetic.

Rick: finally replied. "That has got to be the most profound thing you've ever said. How did you even come up with that?"

"It just came to me. I guess we all have our moments." Chad replied.

Charlie still had a surprised look on his face and asked his brother "Have you been reading encyclopedias again little brother?"

"No, I'm just not as dumb as you look."

Charlie replied back. "If that's true, then someone please wake me up from my dream."

Rick: smiled at his friends and all he could say to them was "You know that's the absolute truth. The journey in life is just *the Music of Life.*" Everybody just started smiling and laughing because he was right. Then they got back to their usual routine of harassing each other as friends and family do. They

went back to what was best about being
friends; they could be who they really were
without judgment and Bud could be
surrounded by the laughter of people that
were happy instead of filled with the dismal
despair of those looking for a way out. Bud
could be surrounded by his family because
that's what they all were to each other – it was
part of their Music of Life.

∞∞∞∞∞∞∞∞∞∞

Rick continued to sit at the piano
staring at the picture and reading the letter
over and over. People started to arrive at the
club and Rick was supposed to be preparing
for his first set, but he couldn't take his eyes
off the picture. He had a saddened look on his
face, but then he began to smile.
Bud was still stocking beer in the bar.
Susan, Charlie, Chad and Old Man
Henderson were at the bar in their usual
places. Susan was behind the bar helping
Bud having some whimsical conversation with
the usual gang. Bud looked at Rick and then
looked at the rest of the gang. He said to them
"Everybody don't bother Rick for awhile, he

got another letter from Liz." They all nodded and left Rick alone, but they were never too far off if he needed them.

Rick still looking at the picture thought to himself you know Liz, he was right.-the journey we take in life is definitely *The Music of Life.* He couldn't help but smile at the strange sense of fate where doing the right thing usually means doing an unselfish act of kindness for someone. It also means that we don't always get what we want, but when we are meant to have something true it's always in that perfect time just like a perfect tempo.

Rick looked up at the door for a moment and smiled. Then he put the letter which he had read a dozen times back in the envelope along with the picture of Liz. Then Rick started to play his song inspired by her, *There's Somebody Like You.* It was the song that was deep inside of him, hidden away from everybody else, and it was only love that could bring it out. As he started playing, everybody in the club started to hum the song or sing it out loud to themselves.

Rick just played the piano like he had always did. All he could do was play and live with the truest passion he had in his heart. It was the passion that brought love out of him again and gave him second chances. *The*

Blue's Note, well it was that place, a place that changes lives while giving nourishment to music men and troubadours. For Rick, being there once again changed his life.

As he played his song that reminded him of her he simply smiled. It didn't matter if she ever walked back through the door - his life had been profoundly changed by her and he would be better off because of that. He kept smiling while thinking of his life with all of its complexities and contradictions. They were the notes and he was the tempo, and the life he would live was *the Music of Life*.

There's Somebody like You

Words and Music by Marcus Blake

Jazz: with upbeat and jazzy feeling

1st verse
G7   Cmaj7   Am7\C
There's somebody like you
A7   Em7__A7
Who haunts my dreams
A7   Em7__A7
Who makes me feel real
Fmaj7   A7   Fmaj7   A7
I couldn't laugh and I couldn't sing
A7   D7   G7__C
Without somebody like you

2nd verse

G7   Cmaj7   Am7\C
There's somebody like you
A7   Em7__A7
That I want to wake up to
A7   Em7__A7
That I want to take my fears away
Fmaj7   A7   Fmaj7   A7
Maybe I couldn't be sad, but only glad
A7   D7   G7__C
Perhaps with somebody like you

1st chorus

```
E7                      Am7                     D7
I've waited for so long to meet the right one
E7              Am7             D7
To have an honest chance at true love
Cmaj7                   Am7       Cmaj7          Am7
And I can't tell you why some were made to love
      Gm7\C
and some were not
Cmaj7               Dm7             Fm6
But now I've learned what love is all about
A7              D7              G7__C
Because there's nobody like you.
```

3rd Verse

```
G7              C maj7      Am7\C
I couldn't find anybody like you
A7                          Em7__A7
With a smile that melts my heart away
A7                      Em7__A7
Or can level me with those eyes
Fmaj7           A7          Fmaj7               A7
I've kept searching all this time,  but it's been hard to
find
A7        D7        G7__C
Anybody that's like you
```

4th Verse

```
G7        C maj7        Am7\C
```
With somebody like you
```
A7            Em7__A7
```
It's been safe to say
```
A7            Em7__A7
```
My search is over
```
Fmaj7              A7       Fmaj7              A7
```
I've never had any luck, until I bumped into you
```
A7              D7          G7__C
```
Because there's nobody like you

2nd chorus

```
E7                      Am7                     D7
```
I've waited for so long to meet the right one
```
E7                      Am7                 D7
```
To have an honest chance at true love
```
Cmaj7              Am7       Cmaj7              Am7
```
And I can't tell you why some were made to love
```
  Gm7\C
```
and some were not
```
Cmaj7                Dm7                 Fm6
```
But now I've learned what love is all about
```
A7                D7          G7__C
```
Because there's nobody like you.